THE FINAL STEPS

○ ○ ○ ○

A Harbor Springs Cozy Legal Mystery

by

Mark M. Bello

This book is dedicated to the divine nine, my grandchildren, with all my love . . .

Table of Contents

Prologue

"Tyler, what's wrong?" Rosaline asked, as she approached her friend.

"Something terrible has happened!" Tyler exclaimed, his face pale with shock. "I need your legal insight and assistance. The investigators aren't telling me anything. Hopefully, with your credentials and experience, and without crossing any legal boundaries, you can persuade them to tell me what's going on."

"Investigators?" Rosaline was confused. "What investigators? What are they investigating? What's happened?"

"Come with me, please?" Tyler implored. "I wouldn't bother you for something trivial. This is awful."

They walked together to the other side of the building. That's when Rosaline saw the red and blue flashing lights. Multiple squad cars and an ambulance blocked entry to that side of the building. Yellow crime scene tape surrounded a beautiful outdoor staircase. A body lay at the bottom of the stairs.

"Tyler, what in God's name?

"It's Kevin Johnstone," Tyler blurted. "He's dead!"

Rosaline paused. Did a petty disagreement between colleagues escalate into a man's death? How? Why? Every instinct told her not to involve herself. But Tyler was terrified; she couldn't abandon him.

Rosaline was shaken to her core—she'd just met Johnstone. He was fine—quite charming, in fact. They'd enjoyed an interesting chat. *How can he be dead?* She looked around the area. A few scraps of paper fluttered around, a piece of chipped, pink fingernail, and . . . Rosaline's heartbeat quickened. She saw something suspicious. Her mind drifted back to events that led to this moment, wondering if she missed anything . . . earlier . .

Chapter One

Rosaline Maxwell finished reviewing her notes for the millionth time. She was about to deliver her maiden lecture at the first stop on her book tour, attempting to ignore the voices in her head. *Will anyone bother to listen?*

"You know this material by heart," she muttered aloud. "It's your book. You wrote every word. You did the research."

As a first-time lecturer, she was in a panic. While she had mastered the subject matter, she was not an experienced public speaker. She was once a defense attorney, most recently a judge, used to speaking in a courtroom setting. Her legal and judicial background also qualified her to write a book exploring cases that highlighted flaws in the legal system. Multiple innocent victims spent years in prison because of those flaws. But could she truly lecture competently and confidently on the matter?

There was another important difference from her days in the courtroom. Here, she would not be the judge—she'd be the judged. What if her legal and judicial skills didn't transfer to a lecture format? Plus, there was an unfortunate trend she stumbled upon while writing her book. She discovered that people tended to show considerably more remorse for *victims* of crimes, than they did for people who were first convicted, and then later found innocent. Those victims made people uncomfortable—the subject was almost never well received, and 'innocent until *proven* guilty' had become akin to a myth. Law enforcement, prosecutors, judges, and even the public were slow to embrace changes in the law to favor people merely *accused* of crimes.

"I find it fascinating but will my audience?" she mumbled aloud. "They probably won't hear a single word I have to say."

She took a welcome moment from her growing anxiety and glanced at herself in the dark screen of her phone. Her wavy, brown hair was perfectly tamed. Her green eyes were shielded by a pair of specially chosen glasses. A white business suit gave her an aura of professionalism and power, two qualities that did not always embody who she was under the surface.

"Rosaline, you're up," a young woman advised, words Rosaline was dreading. *Showtime!*

She silently pumped herself up, willing herself onto the stage of the circul'ar auditorium. The rows of red velvet seats were filled, lights bouncing off white walls, reflecting the audience's curious gazes.

A larger than expected crowd caused her a moment's pause—her heart felt like it might beat out of her chest. Was it better to have a larger crowd? Smaller meant less pressure. Were her research and presentation interesting enough?

You're knowledgeable. You have valuable information to share. You're determined. You're confident. Her mind repeated the pep talk as she walked on stage. She sensed her audience glaring at her, the pressure threatening to break her. She stumbled through the introduction, her cheeks burning over words as simple as "hello" or her own name.

"I've never done this before," she admitted to the crowd as she began her lecture. "I'm quite nervous." Her own honesty surprised her, but she decided to lean into it. Besides, she couldn't retract the admission. "Perhaps it's because I'm so passionate about the topic we are about to discuss.

"Flaws in our criminal justice system have resulted in the incarceration of too many innocent victims. Voiceless, honest citizens, trapped in a world where others view them as monsters. Who among us can imagine such trauma? Freedom is precious in America—how can this happen in the land of the free? Worse, can we imagine this happening to us? Impossible, right? So impossible, we tend to ignore the fact that it happens and shun the people who are cursed with such a fate.

"Ladies and gentlemen, I refuse to ignore these cold, hard truths. You shouldn't either. Everyone in this auditorium works hard to pursue liberty and justice. In doing so, however, we must face systemic flaws, examine the problem of the unjustly convicted and . . ."

Rosaline was approaching the most difficult part of her presentation, the topic upon which she received the most pushback, the most controversial topic of her work. People seemed incapable of embracing what she considered a crucial concept.

She began to sweat, stammering, stumbling over her words, experiencing the pressure of advocating for people who were incapable of advocating for themselves, people who society often ignored. She paused, took a breath, and reminded herself: *You can do this!*

"... we must examine the conditions that even those who are guilty face," she continued. "Are sentences and punishments fair? How about our state and federal statutes? Does the accused receive a fair shake? Where is our common humanity? We may label them 'monsters' but they are human beings, and too many of them are innocent. When we approach this topic, we must remember to walk a few steps in their shoes."

She began to calm. *No one has booed me. I'm still here.* She gained confidence as she pressed on, able to effectively deliver the remainder of her presentation. A few fumbles, a *faux pas* or two, some moments of consternation, but she persevered, and the audience was receptive. She finished the lecture with some lighthearted banter and a joke. The audience laughed. Was the joke that funny, or were people desperate for comic relief after the heavy-handed topic? *Who cares? They laughed!*

Her topic was of enormous consequence, but she did not wish to overwhelm. Her 'heart attack moment' came as she uttered the last words of her speech. Initially, a deafening silence, then, hearty applause permitted her to breathe again, genuine enough to suggest that the lecture had gone better than she expected.

Her acute stage fright surprised even her, and she was quite relieved to leave the podium. The backstage buzz helped ease some of her leftover tension. Her screw-ups still played heavily in her mind, something she would have to overcome if she was ever to become a seasoned lecturer.

"You were amazing," Jess Watson, the event coordinator praised, as she approached. Her blue-green eyes were wide with enthusiasm, blonde hair bouncing in front of her face. "A difficult topic, but you presented it in such an engaging and approachable way. That's incredibly commendable."

Rosaline blushed at the praise she hadn't dared hope for, not sure how to respond. She had only prepared for rejection.

"I appreciate the praise," she mumbled, "and the wonderful support. You did a terrific job organizing this event."

"It was my pleasure," Jess replied. "Your presentation was the best we've had in quite some time. You are not only interesting, but *engaging*, as well. The crowd loved you!"

"I wholeheartedly agree," Tyler Guthrie remarked, from a short distance behind them.

Rosaline turned and smiled as her old friend approached, handsome as ever with sun lit brown hair, warm, brown eyes, and towering height that made everyone wonder if he once played basketball. Always kind and approachable, she was comforted by his mere presence.

"Commendable job!" he beamed. "Our students are indeed fortunate, and I am extremely grateful. They learned a lot today and will remember this lecture for years."

At that, Jess left to give the two a chance to catch up. Rosaline felt a bit safer that way and wanted to talk. Anxiety was still running rampant through her body. And Tyler witnessed the whole thing, saw the ways she failed. As her friend, she hoped he might point out all her mistakes and offer corrective criticism.

"I'm so sorry, Tyler. Things didn't go as well as I'd hoped," Rosaline confessed, looking away. "I tried—I really did. But my anxiety got the best of me. It permeated my presentation—I didn't explain things as clearly as I would have liked. I stumbled over words, rambled; I just . . . messed up."

Tyler paused. He didn't respond immediately which made her even more self-conscious. He waited in silence for Rosaline's eyes to meet his. Then, he gave her a reassuring smile.

"Roz, you were amazing," he assured. "Were there moments, here and there, where you appeared nervous? Yes. But this was your first time lecturing to a large audience. Nervousness comes with the territory. It's to be expected. Give yourself a break.

"Honestly, the flaws made your lecture more human. Most students fear public speaking. In fact, that's true of people of all ages. So, you showed a little fear, exposed your humanity. You set a positive example for every student who was ever afraid to give a speech. You demonstrated fear, conquered it, and came out better on the other side. It was an important lesson for the kids.

"Besides, your message was transmitted, loud and clear. This was an impassioned pitch for tragic victims who are too often ignored. You presented these people in a sympathetic way which was incredible to witness. Great job!"

Rosaline could see he was being sincere. No, the presentation had its flaws, but Tyler believed in her, as always. That's why he was her best friend.

"I must confess. I feel like I let you down," she admitted.

"You didn't," he declared. "Besides, after everything you've done for me over the years, it would be impossible for you to disappoint me. You should know this by now. I wouldn't have gotten through college or its afterlife without you."

Tyler produced a pen from his shirt pocket and smiled. She had given it to him a couple of years ago, customized for him, during one of his dark periods. The word *Strength* was written across the side, followed by a semicolon. The semicolon related to a trend, new back then, a symbol to remind those who suffered from suicidal thoughts to celebrate life instead.

He tucked the pen behind his ear in one fluid movement. Only *he* understood its significance. She said nothing but stored the reminder. These friends were there for each other, and she appreciated that simple truth, now more than ever.

"Ditto. I would not have gotten through but for you." Rosaline acknowledged.

She flashed back to their college days when both struggled, she with anxiety and Tyler with depression. They were overwhelmed at times, suffering in solitude, barely making it through.

Then they met, becoming fast friends, both needing a friend to confide in, pour out their souls—before long, they became each other's confidant. They confessed their struggles, their vulnerability, in ways Rosaline had never experienced with anyone else.

They got through school together. While they talked less frequently these days, with many other things going on in their lives, they still found time for regular communication. When they needed a true friend to lean on, they were there for each other.

No matter the distance between them, theirs was an unbreakable bond. He would always be special to her. She would do anything for him. In fact, that's why she agreed to this lecture. It was her first stop on a book tour she hoped would increase her confidence level.

"I hope you feel the power of your success. You've done incredible work; you should be proud. You're a real author now. That's impressive."

"I guess so," she conceded. "Sometimes, I don't feel that way. How's an author supposed to deal with this? I'm still me. This author thing is new, rather foreign to me, hard to accept."

"That's completely understandable," Tyler assured. "Self-doubt will often get the best of us. It's a real struggle, difficult to combat. But fight you must! Otherwise, you'll never taste the joy of success. I'm proud of you. I believe in you. It is high time for you to be proud of and believe in yourself."

Rosaline smiled, taking it all in, internalizing his words. They couldn't change anything immediately. An important mindset shift takes time. She felt better, though, and realized that she did, indeed, have much to be proud of. She should savor the moment.

"I'll try," she promised. "Proud . . . not so nervous, that's the goal. I appreciate you. Now, how have you been? We have time to catch up. How are things going? Tell me everything," she insisted.

Rosaline and Tyler began a detailed conversation about their separate lives. Tyler was president of the university—he was trying to implement change, better the lives of his students. Rosaline was caught up in book stuff and an author's life that she never imagined possible, following her retirement from the bench.

They were happy for each other, enthused about the so-called good things in life. Life was once a huge struggle. They were both proud of the lives they enjoyed today.

The longer they spoke, the better Rosaline felt. As she shared her successes, and Tyler gushed over them, she realized she had much to be happy about. Life in retirement was better than she had ever imagined. It sometimes felt like a dream, but it was quite real, and she was grateful.

The hour was late, others awaited her, and they had to wrap up the conversation. While Rosaline was comfortable talking with Tyler, the point of the tour was to branch out, meet other people, and expand her horizons.

"It was wonderful to see you again," Tyler exclaimed. "Will we have another chance to talk before you leave campus today?"

"I'll find you before I leave," she promised. "It was great to see you. I enjoyed our conversation, particularly the pep talk. I needed it. It helped, more than you know."

As she started to leave, a handsome, late 40's man approached them. Tall, salt and pepper hair and beard, with bright blue eyes, the man had an air of cocky confidence, off-putting to some people. Rosaline dealt with a lot of lawyers just like this guy. Yet, there was something charming, even compelling about the man. He sauntered over to Tyler and Rosaline.

"Rosaline!" he bellowed, as if he'd known her for years. "The famous author blesses our campus with her presence and wisdom. When the administration announced you were coming, I was ecstatic, dying to hear your presentation. You did not disappoint. It was well worth the wait—you were fantastic, inspiring, empowering . . ." He paused, still enthusiastic, searching for additional complimentary words. "Incredible, awesome, delightful."

The way he carried on, an on-looker would have thought Rosaline was famous, and her book a best-seller. While it gained traction with her outreach on social media, sales were quite modest. She was hardly a star. Besides, his reaction was too enthusiastic to be genuine.

"Wow! I'm not worthy," she laughed, a lame imitation of a *Wayne's World* actor. "I'm pleased you enjoyed the lecture."

"Lecture *and* book—both were wonderful," he gushed. "I'm Kevin Johnstone, by the way, a law professor at the school. I teach criminal and civil procedure"

"Pleased to meet you," she blushed, shaking his hand. *Important courses.*

"Yeah, yeah, terrific," Tyler scowled, annoyed. "What do you want, Kevin?"

Rosaline was surprised by Tyler's tone and demeanor. He was usually warm, friendly, approachable, and wonderful with people, the main reason for his success. She barely recognized *this* Tyler, cold and rude towards this law professor. He obviously detested Kevin Johnstone.

"What's your problem, man? Must I want something?" Kevin retorted, annoyed by Tyler's rude behavior. "I'm a fan of her work. I just wanted to introduce myself to an author I respect. I've used her text in my classes. Her insights are invaluable. She's a remarkable woman."

Kevin's words did little to assuage Tyler's demeanor and attitude. If possible, he grew more outraged. For some reason, Tyler hated this man, which was unusual, as Tyler got along with everyone.

"We know who you are," Tyler groused. "You're a charmer. A snake oil salesman. Perhaps you can charm Rosaline, but you don't fool me, not for a second. I see right through you. Rosaline will figure out who you really are. She's brilliant, observant, and you don't want to mess with her. So, again, what the hell are you doing here?"

Rosaline was stunned. She stepped back, slightly, retreating, not interested in taking part in such a hostile conversation, wondering if she should just walk away. The obvious tension between these two had nothing to do with her. She surveyed her surroundings, seeking an exit route if one became necessary.

"What is your damage, Tyler? I have no idea what you're so angry about," Kevin grumbled. "Truly, what have I done to offend you? Whatever it is, I sincerely apologize. I never have bad intentions, but I'm sorry if I've said or done anything to upset you."

Kevin turned back to Rosaline, which made her uncomfortable. She was not going to take the side of a stranger in a war of words with her best friend. Clearly, Tyler didn't like him. He was an excellent judge of character. His judgment was an excellent reason to be suspicious of this law professor.

"Rosaline, I'm so sorry you're being dragged into whatever this is," Kevin sighed, dismayed. "I wanted to congratulate you on your accomplishments, your lecture, and the book. I had no idea I would cause such a raucous or I would have stayed away. We don't typically have these sorts of acrimonious confrontations here at the university. I apologize for my involvement, on behalf of the school . . ."

"Shut the hell up, Kevin. Don't even start," Tyler interrupted. "You don't represent this school. Don't apologize on its behalf. You are a terrible example of what our school stands for. I won't let you tarnish its name."

Rosaline remained terribly uncomfortable. She wanted Tyler to let whatever this was go, cease, desist, or continue the discussion out of her presence. Her anxiety level was already high. This confrontation was making things worse.

She was, however, curious. Lawyers are naturally suspicious, questioning everything, sometimes the smallest of details. As much as she decried her involvement, she couldn't help but wonder what made Tyler so furious. What did Kevin do? What would make an otherwise kind person act so rude?

"Exit, stage right, my cue to go," Kevin chuckled, attempting to defuse the situation. "I'm not wanted. You've made that clear, but before I depart, congratulations again, Rosaline. It was a pleasure to read your book and listen to your take on such an important topic. I hope we cross paths again, sometime, and have a chance to talk, become better acquainted."

"Perhaps," Rosaline responded, concerned that being cordial would betray her friendship with Tyler.

Kevin smiled, departed, and left Rosaline and Tyler to commiserate in silence.

Chapter Two

"What the heck, Tyler?" Rosaline challenged, as they watched Kevin disappear.

"I don't want to talk about it," Tyler snarled.

"Come on. You know you can tell me anything. Clearly, something's going on between you two. What is it? I've never seen you behave like this. Where's all this anger coming from?"

"Long story," he sighed. "Kevin's a bad guy. Let's leave it there. He's capable of fooling most people into thinking his intentions are good, even had me fooled, once upon a time. But he's evil personified—sneaky and manipulative. Better to stay away from him. You do not want anything to do with this man."

"That's so vague," Rosaline asserted.

"I know, and I'm sorry. Like they say on the news, details at eleven. I'll explain more once we're off campus. Can we drop it or now? It's honestly not important. Sometimes, in life, we come across people we don't like. For me, Kevin is one of those people."

Tyler glanced at his watch. "Look at the time! I've got to run, a few things to attend to. You should get going too, branching out, meeting new people."

"Except Kevin."

"Except Kevin. Stay as far away from him as possible."

Rosaline watched Tyler walk away in the same direction Kevin traveled a few minutes earlier. She was still uncomfortable, now wondering whether Tyler was about to confront Kevin a second time. She had to put it out of her mind. There was still a book signing to do, and she needed to focus. She was relieved that the confrontation was over for now. She was curious, a lawyer, but not curious enough to involve herself in someone else's feud.

She tried to mingle with the crowd. It was expected and helped remove the drama from her conscious thoughts. She was anxious about mingling, began to engage, and promptly forgot about Kevin and Tyler.

A short time later, Jess approached her. "Time for the next part of your day— the book signing. Aren't you excited?"

She was. A book signing meant potential sales. Sales meant success. However, she couldn't imagine people standing in line, craving her book or autograph. That was for famous people, sports stars, Hollywood types, politicians, and former presidents. She was no big deal, an idiot for agreeing to participate.

Perhaps no one will show up. She'd look stupid and incompetent. If people did show, how would the conversation go? What would she say? What would they say? Was there sufficient interest in her work to justify a book signing?

A sense of imposter syndrome kept her frozen in place. Her thoughts drifted back to Tyler, how complimentary he was, how much he believed in her. And the law professor was even more complimentary. Maybe she was better than she believed. *Hold that thought. Believe in yourself.*

She trailed Jess to the signing table. To her surprise and relief, a line of people awaited her approach. *Book sales!* People saw her coming and began to applaud. Eager students held her masterpiece in hand, anxious for her dedication and signature. *This is surreal!*

Ironically, Rosaline had no intention of being a published author. A good friend, Alexis, stole the manuscript off her desk and submitted it behind her back. Rosaline was passionate about her work, eager to discuss it, and Alexis believed it was an important book. She secretly copied the manuscript and sent it to an agent. To everyone's surprise, except, perhaps, Alexis, Rosaline received an offer she couldn't refuse. Besides, this was secretly what she always wanted, but never thought possible.

Yet here she was, an author with a line of people who bought her book and awaited her signature. Rosaline reminded herself that she had made it this far. Her readers were here, she was here. She needed to have confidence, appreciate and enjoy her ten minutes of fame. She was fulfilling a dream. Why not enjoy the moment?

A new sense of strength pulsated through her as she approached the signing table. She sat down. Jess invited the first in line to come forward. The initial conversation was easy and enjoyable. Rosaline began to relax, signing books, and taking photos with fans eager to discuss her work. The tension evaporated. Her passion took over. It was easy to discuss that which she was passionate about. She was surprised at the number of readers who shared her concerns. She didn't expect this, and it made her far more comfortable and fulfilled.

"I'd love an autograph and picture," a middle-aged woman requested, one of many who echoed the same request.

"Of course," Rosaline agreed. "Your enthusiastic support is much appreciated."

"I look forward to reading the book, but I am not a fan," the woman clarified, stiffly, offended by the insinuation. "I have real issues with the positions you espouse. People in jail, for the most part, deserve to be there. We don't need to coddle criminals. To hell with leniency. Victims matter most. They must have justice. If a few criminals are over-sentenced, so be it. They chose a life of crime."

Rosaline froze. This reaction aggravated her. There were many people who agreed with this woman.

"I'm here for my daughter. The book and the photo are presents," the woman continued. "She believes in your research and findings. She's a huge fan. When she heard you were going to lecture near my home, she begged me to come, buy your book, and grab your autograph. Wait until she sees this photo! There isn't much I wouldn't do for her. This was an easy decision."

Rosaline was at a loss for words. *The nerve of this woman!* The novice author didn't wish to make a scene, but she felt slighted at her own event. Who rains on someone's parade like that? She wanted to engage with the woman, convince her of her superior wisdom on the subject, and prove the woman wrong. Instead, Rosaline wisely took the photograph and signed the book, pleased that the dedication was for the *daughter*, someone who believed in her philosophy.

The woman moved on, but the words replayed in Rosaline's mind. All her doubts bubbled to the surface. Was she good enough? Did she have the right to call herself an 'expert?' Why were people waiting in line for her work? She was no big deal. Perhaps she should have tried to change the woman's mind. Or, maybe, just maybe, she wasn't the best woman to advocate for justice for the wrongfully convicted, incarcerated, or overcharged. Maybe she never would be.

She pressed on, less confident than before her encounter with the woman. A young college student, probably a freshman or sophomore, approached the table. Her blue eyes were bright with enthusiasm. With her dark hair and pale complexion, the young woman looked like a real-life version of Snow White.

"It's wonderful to meet you," the girl gushed. "I'm Lindsey, your *biggest* fan."

Rosaline was taken aback by this. Was she popular enough to have a 'biggest' fan? Most of her book signing attendees were cordial, some even enthusiastic, but this was a bit over the top.

"I'm just in awe of your work," Lindsey effused. "Such an important issue and your insights are fresh and revolutionary. You're doing solid work. It's admirable. I look up to you *so much*," she continued to rave.

This was a big shift from her last interaction—while Rosaline weighed her response, she decided to mask her uncertainty with a smile.

"I so appreciate your support," Rosaline chirped, as Lindsey handed the book over for Rosaline's signature and dedication. "My work would have no impact, if not for loyal and enthusiastic readers like you. People who earnestly consider these injustices must ignite the fuel for change."

"Let's hope so," Lindsey agreed. "That's the best part of your writing. It helps me believe that an average citizen can be an agent for change. If I got involved, I might further the cause. It is . . . *inspiring*.

"As I pursue my degree, someone like you comes along and reminds me that I can aspire to a career or venture that makes a difference. There is power in our voices and our advocacy. I want to be like you, someone who strives to create positive change in the world."

Rosaline, initially flattered, was now uncomfortable. She appreciated the kind words, but Lindsey's fandom was too much. Rosaline's insecurity reared its ugly head. Her lack of self-esteem caused her to think that Lindsey's compliments were undeserved. In her own mind, Rosaline simply told stories of injustice and people struggling or treated poorly. She sought to provide a voice to the voiceless . . .

Lindsey startled her out of her thoughts. "Do you think you'll ever write fiction?" Lindsey queried.

"Actually, I'm working on that," Rosaline confided.

She'd been working on a murder mystery for quite some time, a fictional account of her own story. She hadn't gotten very far; the thought was terrifying, far more intimidating than giving a lecture or attending a book signing.

"You must share all the details! This is *so* exciting," Lindsey carried on.

The young student was overstepping the usual time allotted to exchange pleasantries, dedicate, sign, and move on. Rosaline tried to spend some 'personal time' with each reader, but this was beyond that. People in line were murmuring their discontent. She had to keep the line moving, prevent anyone from having to wait too long.

"Follow me on social media. There's more to come," Rosaline chuckled with a shrug. "Wouldn't want to ruin the surprise now, would we?"

Lindsey nodded, a bit disappointed. "Clever lady. Create suspense. Work your fans up until they're primed to purchase. Excellent strategy. I can't wait to read it!"

"Would you like a picture together?" Rosaline suggested.

Lindsey jumped at the opportunity, excited to take a photo with her hero. Rosaline was sure of one thing—Lindsey *was* her biggest fan. Lindsey tried to ask more questions, but Jess rescued Rosaline by calling for the next in line. Impatient people were about ready to walk.

The remaining attendees never reached the dramatic level of attention Lindsey provided, but there were interesting snippets of conversation. Rosaline enjoyed meeting people who were interested in and appreciated her work. She never imagined being given an opportunity to connect with people on this level. She soaked it all in and tried to enjoy every minute of it, fearing it might magically disappear.

It did not disappear, however, and by the time the book signing was over, she was totally drained. She did not awaken from some magical dream. This was real, too real in some ways, with way too much pressure for her taste.

After all the attention, she left the school building, rather unfulfilled. She was apprehensive about the future. Things went well today, which somewhat assuaged her fears, but this was a book tour. She had multiple engagements to attend in multiple venues. Would they all go this well? Would she screw some up? Would her anxiety and self-loathing defeat her? Or would these events become easier as she went along?

Rosaline wanted to see Tyler again, before leaving the campus, but needed time to process the events of the day. How did she critique her own performance and the audience's reaction? Too much pressure? How did she handle it? Would it be easier or more difficult in the future? Her old self-doubts bubbled to the surface.

She headed to her RV, sniffing the air, noting the fall air scent, wrapping around her like a cozy, September sweater. Colorful leaves painted the campus with hope for people following their dreams. A quiet peace settled over the elderly brick buildings, marking late afternoon passage into evening, as students finished classes for the day.

As she neared the RV, she reflected on the strangeness of life in a constantly moving home. She would live in a home that rode from place to place, transporting her to new and unique locations, to meet thousands of people on a book tour. It was the most adventurous thing she'd ever done. She was still nervous, anxious to move on, excited that the first event was over.

She paused and sat down on a bench situated under a huge, leafy maple tree. She sighed, thinking how strange it was to be retired, after a long legal and judicial career. She'd had a successful career, first as a lawyer, then as a circuit court judge. Obviously, her peers thought enough of her to recommend her initial appointment to the circuit bench. Afterward, the voters were impressed enough to re-elect her multiple times. She was confident in that skill set. A comfortable old shoe. She had no problem socializing with lawyers, citizens, politicians, and other judges, in that environment.

This author's stuff was different, a whole new experience. *Am I truly ready for this?*

"I don't know," she whispered aloud, glancing around, hoping no one heard her talking to herself. "Who knows what's to come? All I know is that I must do this. I must rise to the challenge."

After all, she spent a fortune on an RV and had chosen the venues to visit. She could not disappoint the people who put all this together or readers who wanted to meet and greet her. The issues were important, as was alerting and educating the public. Besides, there was the issue of money. She had a decent retirement account and a judicial pension. Social Security would be the maximum benefit, but her book was essential to achieving her retirement goals. Its success would make a huge difference in her golden years. There was no backing out or backing down. She had to figure out a way to deal with her anxiety and all the attention.

She decided to tackle this, tune out her insecurities, gather all her strength and, as the *Nike* commercials say, 'just do it.' She might change lives, even *save* lives with her work. She was born for this.

Rosaline rose and began to walk toward the RV. As she approached the threshold, a familiar voice stopped her.

"Rosaline!" he called. "Before you go, I need to talk to you. It's urgent!"

Rosaline turned to Tyler. She considered extending an apology for intending to leave campus without saying goodbye. Perhaps she'd invite him to dinner, her treat, do something, *anything*, to excuse her rudeness. But something was wrong. Tyler's face was strangely contorted—he needed help. Suddenly, everything else was forgotten. Nothing else mattered.

Chapter Three

Rosaline's thoughts returned from the earlier events of the day to Tyler's current, very tragic, and scary circumstances. How did things change so quickly? A man died on campus. Rosaline and Tyler walked, side by side, inching over to the building. The yellow crime scene tape impeded their path to the staircase. Security was guarding the premises, keeping onlookers from entering. Tyler, however, was the school's president, and the guards lifted the tape. He and Rosaline ducked under and through but were not permitted to approach the body.

"He must've fallen," Rosaline surmised, sickened by the sight of blood dripping down the staircase, pooling on the floor.

"Not exactly," Tyler responded. "According to the detectives on the scene, the way his body is positioned, they believe he was standing with his back to the stairs. That would mean he was pushed. His head cracked against the cement, causing his death."

"So, he . . . they . . . believe this was intentional?" Rosaline whispered.

"Yes." Tyler nodded. "That seems to be the case."

Rosaline once handled such cases as an attorney. She also presided over several as a judge. But it had been a while, and she never expected to be involved in a murder case, post-retirement. They always left her with nightmares and headaches, the details lingering in her mind, long after the cases were concluded.

She was retired and wanted no part of a murder or murder investigation. She'd left that life behind.

However, the legal and judicial juices began to flow, and she couldn't resist the temptation to evaluate the scene, analytically, as a criminal defense lawyer, cop, or trained sleuth might. The stairwell looked typical, aside from the pooled blood. Those scraps of paper still fluttered about, a piece of chipped fingernail, and that suspicious item . . . the pen.

"Is that your pen, Tyler?" Rosaline gestured toward a pen lying in the blood pool near the body.

She faced Tyler and saw only guilt. His face contorted and he shifted uncomfortably. Rosaline felt like reading him his rights. It *was* his pen, and she didn't wish to hear his answer.

"I think so," he waffled. "At least, it looks like mine. It's difficult to tell at this distance, with all that blood."

But Rosaline was positive it was Tyler's pen, the unusual shade of blue that she spent so much time choosing, determined to buy the perfect gift for him. She purchased it during a particularly rough time in his life. It had to be unique, perfect, and it was. She'd never seen another quite like it. A pen wouldn't fix what ailed Tyler at the time, but she wanted it to serve as a constant reminder that he had a caring friend out there, someone to count on when he felt isolated. Now, it might stand as something else, an ominous sign of something too terrible to consider.

"It's yours," she insisted, irritated and suspicious that he would try to deny it. "I can see, quite clearly, that it's yours."

"Perhaps it fell out of my pocket earlier today. Maybe this morning when I headed for your lecture."

"But you had it while we were talking," she reminded him.

She wanted to let this go. She dreaded the obvious conclusion. She wondered why she pressed the issue. Tyler was incapable of doing the unspeakable . . .

Her mind flickered back to Tyler and Kevin's interaction. Was there something she missed? Or was it so obvious that it was haunting? The tension between them was palpable, more so for Tyler.

"Yes . . ." he said slowly. "I suppose I did. I must've dropped it after the lecture. What are you driving at, Rosaline? I'm not sure I like your tone or the look on your face right now."

Rosaline agreed. She didn't like the way she was feeling either. She didn't like asking these questions or being suspicious of him. Yet, she couldn't turn away from the obvious, just because it made her uncomfortable. After all, it might be crucial evidence in a criminal inquiry.

"It's your pen, Tyler," she concluded. "Smack dab in the middle of a crime scene—right near the body. On top of that, you obviously had issues with the man. You clearly didn't like him much . . ."

Tyler was visibly horrified by what Rosaline was suggesting. So was Rosaline. But her legal training and acumen would not permit her to ignore the obvious.

"What are you insinuating?" Tyler grumbled, eyebrows raised, arms crossed over his chest.

"I'm not insinuating anything," Rosaline insisted. "I'm just curious why your pen is sitting there."

"I didn't harm Kevin, Rosaline," Tyler retorted with a straight face. "I can only come to the unfortunate conclusion that I dropped the pen at the very spot where the crime occurred, or worse, that someone placed it there." His eyes steeled a genuine expression that caused Rosaline to believe his words. Tyler was, typically, an honest man. "I'm not capable of *killing* someone, even a man I didn't like. You know better. I'm not . . ." He lowered his voice to a whisper. "I'm not a murderer."

"I know, Tyler," Rosaline conceded. "I just . . ."

Tyler had denied guilt, out loud, with that look on his face. Rosaline had to confront the darkness of her suspicions. If she truly believed that Tyler's pen meant he had something to do with Kevin's body lying at the bottom of this staircase, she must also believe him capable of murder. The Tyler she remembered was incapable of this level of brutality. So, she concluded, he dropped the pen at an unfortunate location at an unfortunate time but had nothing to do with the crime.

"I'm sorry," she relented. "I know you had nothing to do with it. The finer details of a crime have always been my thing. I'm prone to look for clues. I was just reacting to what I saw."

"I understand your point," Tyler admitted. "And why you have questions . . ." He paused, looking incredibly weary, like the weight of the world was hanging over him. "I-I can't explain why my pen is here . . ."

"Did I hear you correctly, sir. That is *your* pen?" A detective overheard Rosaline and Tyler's conversation. He confronted Tyler.

Rosaline and Tyler exchanged an uneasy glance. They were so focused on their own exchange they ignored the possibility that others were near enough to overhear their words. Rosaline felt guilty for bringing the whole thing to light.

She convinced herself it wouldn't matter. Surely, Tyler had a perfectly rational explanation for presence of the pen. Or perhaps he had a solid alibi. Either way, he was innocent.

Tyler cleared his throat. "Yes, it is," Tyler admitted. "From this distance, it appears to be my pen."

The detective eyeballed him with suspicion. "It's been found at the scene. It's evidence. Obviously, we can't return to you at this time."

"I completely understand," Tyler assented. "Makes total sense. Keep it for as long as you need."

"A few questions, sir?" The detective continued. "You're Tyler Guthrie, right? President of the school?"

"Yes," Tyler advised.

"I'm Detective Remer. I'm the lead detective on this case. I suspect this won't be the last time we talk. May I ask, sir, how did your pen land in the middle of a murder scene?"

Tyler tensed. Rosaline worried he might lie. What if he lied? Was it her civic duty to point out the lie? *Why didn't I rush to the RV and vamoose ten minutes earlier?* She didn't want anything to do with a case that involved her friend. She had to stay, however. Someone had to protect Tyler.

"This is a popular campus location. I am constantly on this stairwell, day-to-day, and I am certain I was on it earlier today," Tyler explained. "The pen must've dropped out of my pocket. It's also possible I had it tucked behind my ear. Probably fell as I walked by."

Rosaline wondered what time Tyler was in the stairwell. Was it near in time to Kevin's murder? Despite the fact she couldn't fathom Tyler offing someone, she also couldn't rid her mind of these suspicious thoughts.

"The deceased was a law professor here, true? What was your relationship with him?" Remer queried. "You're the president of the school—I presume you the two of you friends, colleagues, what?"

Tyler shifted uncomfortably. Rosaline hung on his response. Would Tyler downplay facts that would cause investigators to be suspicious? It must be tempting to lie, twist the truth, perhaps, just a tad. Again, she felt conflicted. She saw the animosity Tyler felt for Kevin. They didn't get along. Might Tyler incriminate himself? She felt a desire to cut off the questioning. What were her responsibilities in this situation? Should she intervene?

If he failed to tell the truth, would she have to be truthful? Would she be forced to turn against her friend? She was no longer a judge, but her morals and ethics hadn't changed.

"We were colleagues, I guess. I didn't like or respect the man," Tyler confessed. "We didn't always see eye-to-eye. We had different morals and perspectives, things we disagreed on. In fact . . ."

Tyler glanced at Rosaline. *What would he say next?* While she worried about pre-judging him, he seemed worried he might be pre-judged. Was he keeping something from her?

". . . Kevin and I had a disagreement earlier today," Tyler admitted. "After Rosaline's lecture. We got into an argument, right near this stairwell. It got a bit heated. Might have been overheard by others. It happened in front of Rosaline. She's a witness. The pen probably dropped out then. The argument was never physical. Rosaline can attest to that. And Kevin was alive and well when we last saw him. Rosaline can attest to that, too."

Remer was not pacified. In fact, he was quite suspicious. Rosaline understood. If she didn't know Tyler . . . when she saw the pen . . . *she* was suspicious. His pen, sitting in the middle of the crime scene, was quite suspicious.

"I think Tyler's said enough," Rosaline interrupted, aware of where the conversation might be headed. "I know Tyler quite well—he had nothing to do with this. If you have additional questions, I recommend that Tyler obtain counsel and that you question him in the presence of his lawyer."

Shock registered on Tyler's face. He never actually considered the possibility that he might be a suspect, even to a cop who didn't know him. Why would he need a lawyer? But his good friend Rosaline Maxwell was telling him to shut his mouth. As a matter of fact, talking to cops without an attorney present, rarely worked in a suspect's favor.

"Who are you, again?" Remer crossed his arms over his chest, glaring at her, awaiting her answer.

"An old college friend," Rosaline advised. "A lawyer and a retired circuit court judge. I know Tyler. I can vouch for Tyler. I also know how you guys think. I know my word won't mean much to you in the general scheme of things, but I want to assure that this man's rights are protected."

"Wise of you to do so," Remer admitted, disappointed. He turned back to Tyler. "I'd like to bring you down to the station for additional questioning. As your friend suggests, you are welcome to have a lawyer present, but this isn't a request. I hope you'll go willingly . . ."

"Of course, I'll go willingly," Tyler interrupted. "I intend to cooperate fully. If Kevin was murdered, I want whoever committed the crime brought to justice. I had nothing to do with this. Let's finish this so you can focus on identifying the *real* killer."

Rosaline interjected. "He needs some time to obtain counsel, Detective. Why don't you do this tomorrow?"

Remer grunted. "I want him down at headquarters as soon as possible. You're a lawyer. You come down with him. One way or the other, he's going down to the station. Do I have to drive him there myself?"

"Not necessary," Tyler assured. "I'll be at the station in the morning. Rosaline will accompany me."

Rosaline looked stunned.

"Come on, Rosaline. You'll come, won't you? We can call another lawyer if this thing goes any further. Please? You'll stay, won't you?" Tyler pleaded as he and Rosaline walked back across the campus. The colorful fall leaves reminded her of the flames Tyler was asking her to extinguish.

"I'm sure we can sort this out. I had nothing to do with this. But I'd be lying if I said I'm not terrified. I need you, Rosaline. You're the best lawyer I know. I need your help. Please, just a while longer? Help me through this."

"I've got commitments, Tyler. The book tour, all those people counting on me. I'm not sure I can stay . . ." Rosaline explained. "I can't believe this is happening to you. I haven't practiced law in years. I don't know how to respond. If you're charged, which appears possible at this moment, you're going to need the best of the best, a lawyer who tries these cases."

"I understand. I know you have the book tour and everything. Come with me to the station. You won't have to stay for long. If the police decide I did it, they won't properly investigate. They won't consider others and won't find the actual perpetrator. I *need* you, Rosaline, now more than ever. We may have to do some digging on our own. We were quite a team in college, remember?

"After this interrogation, help me find the best lawyer around. I'll still need your friendship and legal opinion. I don't want to miss anything or make any mistakes. I don't just want to prove my innocence, there may be a vicious predator on my campus. My kids may be in danger."

Rosaline considered his dilemma. She studied his face. He wore an expression of open honesty, revealing a vulnerability she'd rarely seen in him. She was hooked. She considered how he was during his darker days, how worried she was back then. Would a murder probe send him spiraling again?

"Okay, Tyler, I'll stay," she assented. "As long as possible. However, I must return to my book tour."

"Of course. I can't tell you how much I appreciate you doing this for me."

"You are a treasured friend. How can I not?"

They embraced before Tyler got into his car and drove off. Rosaline's heart sank as she watched him disappear in the distance. Rosaline was acutely aware of how cops thought. Once they focused on a suspect . . . she had little time. She promised to stay. She'd fulfill her promise, but what could she really do?

Chapter Four

osaline's mind was churning as she drove the RV away from the chic college town and back to Harbor Springs. She hadn't intended to spend the night in the northern Michigan resort town, but Tyler's situation demanded her presence. Besides, there was something reassuring about returning to the known and comfortable, after a turbulent and uncomfortable day.

Red and orange leaves of oak and maple trees, nestled among pine needles, created a brilliant and beautiful scene to end a long day. The colors united with a gorgeous sunset, spread across the sky, an extravagant display of nature's wealth, far beyond any human ability. As she continued to drive, a familiar lake came into view, blue waters that captured and held many fond memories.

Twenty minutes later, she reached her lakeside home, a comfortable extravagance that she worked long and hard to afford.

The log lodge was larger and roomier than one person required, but still captured that northern Michigan, rustic feeling.

The garden she worried about leaving was still bright with enthusiasm as fall fell upon her beloved plants. Though she hired a gardener to attend to her pride and joy while she was gone, she was happy to spend additional time caring for it herself.

She walked up to the ornate door and let herself in. Her nose caught a slight aroma of chocolate and vanilla as she turned the lights on, remnants of the cookies she made (and quickly ate) for her trip.

The simplistic décor was spotless, a tribute to her obsession for keeping the house in the best shape possible. It was comforting to be home again. She passed the white and light blue furniture and glanced out at the deck overlooking the lake.

The lake was calm and inviting, but it was too chilly to be out at night. There was no food in her refrigerator, so she ordered a delivery and waited anxiously for it to arrive. Then, she went upstairs to the master bedroom.

She didn't usually eat up there, but, on this night, she craved the additional comfort. She walked to her plush, canopy bed, its white and silver coverings, and snuggled under the covers. She stared at the sky through a skylight in the ceiling. It was her favorite view, a glorious kaleidoscope of blues, spotted with freckles of bright white, clustered in various forms, celebrated for centuries by millions who came before this private moment.

"Please, be okay, Tyler," she whispered.

She had barely finished her food when her cellphone rang. The screen registered an unknown number. Typically, a crank or spam call that Rosaline would let go to voicemail, but considering her unusual day, she decided to answer.

"Rosaline?" It was Tyler's voice, wrought with worry. "I need you. I've been arrested."

Apparently, Tyler was assigned an attorney appointed by the court. The lawyer was helping him, she didn't need to rush to the station. After a short, rather difficult conversation with Tyler, Rosaline struggled to sleep. All she thought about was the following morning, lending her expertise and advice to Tyler, setting the Harbor Spring Police Department straight.

As a law student, Rosaline was naïve. She and many of her classmates believed that trials were 'Perry Mason' events. Truth and justice would always prevail, the criminal would confess or be convicted. The innocent would be exonerated. Years later, a retired lawyer and judge, she still believed in justice, but was convinced that the country needed charging and sentencing reforms. Justice was less frequently blind.

Law enforcement, judges, and juries sometimes freed the wrongdoers and convicted the innocent. Everything was not always fair, and she could not tell Tyler that everything would be fine. She desperately wanted to tell Tyler, if he was innocent, that he would not be punished. The truth would set him free—the real killer would be brought to justice. Those were the ideals she always strived to uphold.

But Rosaline was an author on a book tour. She wrote and lectured about a book that studied inadequacies in our federal and state courts. She had *zero* confidence that truth might prevent an injustice from occurring in Tyler's case. Innocent people were charged, tried, convicted, and punished for things they didn't do. It happened all too frequently. She prayed this wouldn't be the case with Tyler. However, his pen was found at the scene. He clearly detested the victim and had an argument with him on the day of the murder. He was an obvious suspect. Things did not bode well for a finding of innocence.

How might she best help him? The department focused on and charged Tyler. They would not consider alternate suspects. Perhaps her best contribution would be for her to become personally involved. She was a lawyer and judge, not an investigator. What sleuthing skills did she have? As an 'investigator' who was certain Tyler was innocent, perhaps she might see things the detectives wouldn't look for. The cops decided Tyler was the perpetrator. In contrast, Rosaline would be his safety net.

Still, she doubted her capabilities. While she was an expert in the law, she was not a detective. Self-doubt flooded her brain, as usual, only this time there was an overriding concern. Tyler was always there for her, helped to keep her afloat in her worst of times. This was the worst moment of his life. She had to stick with him, stick with the case. She had to act.

She tried her best to sleep. When sleep finally came, it was too quickly interrupted by her phone alarm, alerting her to the fact that it was time to head for the station. She shattered all RV speed records, luckily avoided all state and local radar traps, and drove straight to headquarters. Using her judicial connections, she was escorted to a conference room used for confidential conversations between suspects and their lawyers.

Tyler's physical appearance was sad and shocking. His color was drained, he looked exhausted and defeated, wearing the rumpled clothes he wore the day before. Rosaline was near tears, heartbroken. In less than twenty-four hours, his spirits were at rock-bottom.

"What happened?" Rosaline queried, as gently as possible.

They sat face-to-face across a cold, metal table. Plain, grey walls surrounded them. A too-bright light illuminated the heavy toll the experience was taking on Tyler. He shifted uncomfortably in his seat.

"I don't know," Tyler groaned. "I don't know anything. They came to my home—said they would not wait until morning. I told them you were gone for the evening. A cop asked if I formally retained you as my lawyer. I told him I had not. He asked if I was willing to answer questions without a lawyer. I told him I would not do that. Another cop indicated that a judge would assign me a lawyer.

"They dragged me down to the station. The lawyer was there. He told me I didn't have to answer any questions, had the right to remain silent, *Miranda* and all that, but the cops would probably arrest me and throw me in jail if I didn't cooperate. So, against my lawyer's advice, I decided to talk to Detective Remer, tell him the truth, the whole truth, and nothing but the truth. My reward for my cooperation and honesty? These jerks throw me in the slammer! I didn't like the guy, Roz, it's true. But I didn't *kill* him. They must know that. Surely, *you* know that!"

Rosaline was concerned. Tyler confessed to disliking the victim. He confessed to a verbal altercation. His pen was found at the scene. Rosaline witnessed all three of these things. These simple facts would present problems for his defense. In fact, it was an easy circumstantial case, enough to convince anyone who didn't know Tyler, that he was guilty of murder.

"Always listen to your lawyer," she chided. "The truth is subject to interpretation and can sometimes cause a suspect as much trouble as a lie. This is a completely private room. We can talk without anyone listening. Start at the beginning. Perhaps I can help, listen to your story, pick it apart. Identify bits of reasonable doubt. With luck, I might actually solve this thing and bring the real murderer to justice. I have to try."

"What can I do from a jail cell?" Tyler whimpered, utterly defeated.

"I'll talk to your lawyer. Try to arrange bail. I'll even post, if I must. But it won't matter where you are," Rosaline promised. "I will be here for you no matter what. Now, talk to me, why didn't you like Kevin?"

"It's complicated," Tyler began, "and as simple as the answer I gave Remer. You heard what I said. We have different morals, as in I have them, and he didn't."

Rosaline flinched. An answer like that meant trouble for Tyler. Talking trash about the victim is not a winning argument for a murder suspect. Any cop or prosecutor would pounce on it.

"I could write a novel full of Kevin's bad deeds," Tyler continued, working himself up a bit too much. "Think of every bad quality you can find in a guy. That's Kevin. Selfish, rude, sneaky, manipulative, a liar—he was just a terrible person.

"I'm sorry he died. I'm sad to speak ill of the dead. But his death doesn't change the truth. He was a terrible human being. I'm sorry, but it's true."

Rosaline looked away. She presided over enough cases to know that there are two sides to every story. A perp is not always pure evil. A victim is not always a pleasant person. There are grey areas. Still, it was discomforting to know that Tyler said these things to the cops about a victim he stands accused of killing.

She paused, clearing her head, trying to think like a lawyer.

"This might turn out to be a positive," Rosaline reasoned. "If Kevin was as bad as you say, there must be others who disliked him. Perhaps there were others he crossed. Some might have a motive for murder."

"There is absolutely no question of that important truth," Tyler fumed, a look of pure hatred in his eyes. "Of *course*, he upset a lot of people, including colleagues, friends, and family. They were his favorite targets."

"That's wonderful, Tyler! It provides us with a number of alternate suspects." Rosaline was hopeful, for the first time since Tyler called her to advise of his arrest. "Do you have names? Do you know these people? Who did he upset? What were the circumstances? When searching for and evaluating suspects, who should I look at first?"

"Excellent questions," Tyler considered. "I knew the guy well enough to know I didn't want much to do with him. Ever. I preferred to avoid him as much as possible, looking forward to the day I'd find enough evidence to terminate his ass."

Rosaline shuddered. Every time Tyler opened his mouth, he sounded like he hated this guy enough to kill him. She appreciated his honesty, but he was *too* honest. It led to his arrest. If it continued, it might lead to his conviction.

"Start with his wife. Obviously, she knows him better than I do," Tyler suggested. "I doubt they had a solid marriage. She's the perfect alternate suspect. Isn't it always the spouse? That's what they say on television. At the very least, she'd know his enemies. I'm sure she's caught him in all sorts of lies. They were probably heading straight for divorce court."

"Good thinking," Rosaline agreed. "And you're correct. It happens far too often. Marriages may become nasty, violent, and even deadly, while couples await the consequences of divorce. Love and hate are equally powerful emotions. A marriage in turmoil is often a motive for murder."

Might the widow have a motive? Rosaline intended to investigate that angle. It was at least as compelling as a colleague or boss who simply didn't like the guy. The more she considered the number of people who disliked someone but would never murder that person, the more she was convinced of Tyler's innocence. At the very least, Kevin's wife had to know something about him or another potential suspect, some juicy morsel that might lead the authorities to a different conclusion. Rosaline had to wonder though: If the couple was heading for a divorce, just before the murder, might that cause the widow to be dishonest? Time would tell.

"I'll find her and try to talk with her," Rosaline promised. "Let me know if you think of any other suspects. In the meantime, and I say this in the politest way possible; shut the hell up! Don't talk to anyone other than me or your lawyer. I will do everything in my power to find the truth, but you can't keep running your mouth off like this. This brutal honesty will be your downfall. Cut it out, *capisce*?"

"*Capisce*," Tyler vowed. "I'll behave. I really do appreciate this, more than you know. I know you've got the book tour."

"Forget the book tour. It's no longer a priority. What matters now is exposing the truth and persuading the cops to focus their efforts elsewhere. I'll focus on my lectures, book, and crusade later. Besides, you'd do the same for me. Do you, by chance, have Kevin's wife's contact information?"

"If you go into my office, all of my faculty contacts are there. There are files for each staff member. I'll release my keys to you. You'll have access to everything the detectives don't take."

"If the detectives took stuff, your lawyer will be able to see what they took through discovery. I'll do my best," Rosaline assured. "Stay positive. We will muddle through this somehow."

"Wow! Thanks! I feel so much better, so much more hopeful."

"I'm glad. Hang in there."

They chatted for a few minutes before Rosaline left to claim Tyler's things and begin clearing his good name.

Chapter Five

Rosaline tried to keep a clear head as she left the station, but she was too distraught. Her experience as a judge and an attorney made things a bit easier. For instance, she understood what to expect from the courtroom, the kinds of things a judge might consider when reviewing the evidence. She wasn't a complete novice like the other campus observers.

Experienced or not, it was difficult to see someone she loved behind bars. And Tyler looked *terrible*, like prison life was already wearing him down. What would he look like after formal charges were filed, he couldn't make bail, and he had to spend the whole pre-trial and trial period in jail? What if he got convicted? Perhaps once the initial shock wore off, he'd regain characteristics of the old Tyler. Or, his appearance and demeanor might worsen as time passed. She shuddered at the thought.

Tyler's mental health was fragile before this nightmare. This was a major challenge of the case. Rosaline was not only fighting for Tyler's freedom but his life, as well. She was convinced he would not do well in lock-up—before long, something terrible would happen. Tyler's long-term fate was imperiled by his mental health concerns.

Rosaline had to solve this case, death, murder, whatever it was. She resolved to do so. She would help Tyler navigate out of this mess, and fix things for him like he had always done for her. She would stay and see this thing through to the end.

Thoughts and worries clouded her mind. She tried to focus, block out all distractions, and consider the evidence. She sucked in a breath and exhaled, slowly, gathering her wits about her. Then, she headed to Tyler's office on campus. Hopefully, she'd find a clue or two in his private space. With luck, she'd find evidence solid enough to make his guilt less likely. She wished to discover something, anything, that would make bail possible. The case would be easier if he was released and could assist in his own defense.

As she strolled toward Tyler's office, the campus seemed different than the other day. Or was she imagining things? The mood was somber, the crime cast a shadow over the tree-sheltered grounds. Stunned students shuffled around, heads down, the news of a murder on campus impacting all. Worse, their professor was the victim—their school's president was accused of the crime. These were unique and troubling circumstances for young students. Rosaline hoped that the administration provided counseling.

Rosaline entered the staff office building. Professors and staff were chatting with students, trying to wear brave faces. Rosaline sensed their discomfort, shock, and disbelief that this happened on *campus*. She glanced at the elderly men and women as she walked by. Did they know Kevin? Did they like and respect Tyler? Did they believe he was capable of murder? Those who knew either or both had to be reeling at the terrible news. But above all else, she sensed unbridled *fear*. If Tyler was innocent, as almost all suspected, a murderer might still be lurking on campus.

Rosaline was determined to solve the crime, prove her friend innocent, bring a murderer to justice, and restore calm to a panicked community. She reached Tyler's office and stood at the front door, looking about, absorbing curious glances from faculty, staff, and students. She waited until she was alone, before unlocking the door and slipping inside. She quickly shut and locked the door behind her. She'd done nothing wrong but felt a compelling need for discretion.

She sat down at Tyler's desk. Suddenly, it hit her, like a Muhammed Ali twister punch. This is dangerous! Tyler is innocent. The killer is still at large. *Did the killer just pass me by? Does he or she know I'm investigating? Might the killer come after me if I stumble on the truth?* She hugged herself, shuddered, and took a moment to gather herself.

Tyler's office reminded her of . . . well . . . Tyler. In fact, the office was so 'Tyler' she found it difficult to breathe. Awards and plaques adorned the walls. Tokens of his many travel adventures stood proudly on bookcases or filled open spots around his desk. He had an impressive collection of non-fiction books from brilliant minds around the world and an almost equally impressive collection of his favorite novels. His collection brought character to the office. A visitor might begin to know the real Tyler simply by absorbing his personal library. Many novels in Tyler's fictional collection were beloved crime thrillers. The irony of him now being the principal protagonist of his own real life crime thriller weighed heavily on her as she commenced her search for clues.

"Let's make sure the process works for you," Rosaline whispered aloud.

She walked to Tyler's computer and entered the password he provided. She was honored by his trust, knowing that privacy was extremely important to him. She would try to limit her electronic search to items relevant to the case. Tyler insisted he had nothing to hide. That's why he gave Rosaline the password. But this simple act of faith helped her believe even more in his innocence. If he had something to hide, it would likely be stored on his hard drive. Total access to his electronic history made the prospect of his guilt almost minuscule. Tyler was innocent. Everything was on the table if it proved his innocence.

Rosaline rummaged through her purse and extracted a memory stick. The computer, both hardware and software, had to remain behind. Remer's team would soon be duplicating her search. Copying the files allowed her to access them throughout, without having to return to Tyler's office.

She scanned Tyler's files and found one marked 'teacher personnel files.' She searched for and located Kevin's files and copied the information to her memory stick. She would study the files later. For now, she'd scan them, seeking his vital information. She opened the first file. Jackpot! She had Kevin's home address.

She punched the address into her phone's *GPS*, closed all open files, and rose to leave. Dark thoughts caused her to stop in her tracks. She approached this computer search convinced of Tyler's innocence. But what if he was guilty? What if there was damning evidence on the computer files she just copied? What if Tyler was counting on her to look the other way? What if she was caught between her loyalty to Tyler and a charge of aiding and abetting a murderer?

These thoughts now overwhelmed her. She felt dizzy and almost fell into Tyler's executive chair. She sat a moment and composed herself. *Tyler is not a killer!* She decided. But Rosaline Maxwell, judge and lawyer, knew that dangerous people hid dangerous, even murderous tendencies quite well. She'd presided over trials where criminals were found not guilty because they did a terrific job of disguising who and what they were. Justice is blind, and criminals can sometimes blind the most perceptive and righteous people. In many of her criminal cases, there were no signs that the guilty person was capable of committing such horrible deeds.

Evaluating whether or not an accused possesses sufficient *mens rea* for the crime is an important skill in lawyering and judging cases. Rosaline believed herself qualified to make that determination. She had decades of experience to back up her belief. But this case was different. She was not a detached observer in a jury trial, not the trier of fact and law in the bench trial of an accused criminal she'd never met before. This was Tyler. She was human, inherently flawed by bias. Might she be blind to the actions of a loved one?

This was why the truth was so important in this case. No matter where the evidence took her, even if the discoveries caused her discomfort, she had to find the truth. She decided to revisit Tyler's hard drive and computer files to determine, then and there, if there was anything that might help or hang him.

The search was tedious, routine school and personnel stuff that university presidents do each day. Nothing seemed amiss until she found his notes, things he wrote down, so he wouldn't forget them. Most were impersonal, unremarkable bits of information until she saw a note with a now familiar name.

I caught Kevin flirting with a fellow teacher. She seemed uncomfortable with his behavior, so I asked her. She insisted nothing was wrong. Called it 'friendly banter.' Her body language suggested otherwise. Without a complaining witness, I can't prove misconduct. Let it go, this time, but it's clear this guy is a deceitful bastard. Don't want him working for this school anymore. He's more trouble than he's worth. Must protect the students and find a way to dump his sorry ass. Someone formidable is protecting him. Not sure who or why but he always seems to wiggle his way out of trouble. Always one step ahead of me. Frustrating! One way or another he's a problem in need of a solution.

A cold chill cut through Rosaline's body. She shivered as she read and re-read the note. Tyler was investigating Kevin and wanted to fire him. *Not too surprising.* His dislike for the man was clear, not something he tried to hide.

To the cops, however, a written note like this was a solid motive for murder. If Tyler was unable to terminate Kevin through legitimate means, would he resort to *murder*? She knew the answer, but what would the cops think?

Rosaline tried to put friendship aside and look at the evidence impartially, like a judge. Judges aren't allowed to handle trials for best friends—it's a conflict of interest. To what lengths would a school president go if his students were in danger? Would he do whatever possible to protect them? Murder? Did he have some type of hero complex? The cops will think so.

Continuing her judicial analysis, was the note enough? Rosaline didn't believe it was. She was just commencing her private efforts. Investigators may have a thin motive, but there was no proof Tyler murdered Kevin—nothing that proved him guilty beyond a reasonable doubt. There would be other suspects once the investigation heated up. If Kevin was as unpleasant a person as Tyler claimed, others must have wanted him dead. Her focus needed to be on those others because the cops appeared to be focused on Tyler.

She imagined the scenario. They would search the office and find Tyler's notes. It was just a matter of time. She'd dive into Kevin's life, and identify alternate suspects, friends, colleagues, associates, relatives, or others with a solid motive. She downloaded the balance of Tyler's notes to her memory stick and left the office, hoping to soon have a list of alternate suspects to investigate. He didn't do this. It had to be someone else.

Chapter Six

Rosaline was somewhat apprehensive as she drove to Kevin's house. She was quite skilled at asking probing questions in court or querying a prospective client to make sure his or her story made sense, but she had never acted as an investigator. She worried she might miss something or ask the wrong questions. Should she leave Tyler's fate to the locals, let the professionals do the work?

She thought about the many criminal cases she handled as a lawyer and those she presided over as a judge. She was convinced that the detectives would focus on Tyler. Once that happened, they'd be blind to the truth. Cops handle multiple cases at once, a solid suspect results in laziness and causes them to move on to the next case. The detectives in Kevin's case simply were not reliable. She refused to allow Tyler to become one of the many people wrongly convicted of a serious crime. Inexperienced in private sleuthing or not, she had to continue. There was no other option.

Rosaline pulled up to a pleasant looking, well-kept ranch style home, white siding and matching picket fence, a small garden out front, and a lush, green lawn. The home had an open format. As Rosaline walked up the path to the front door, she could see through the house to a play area, pool, deck, and barbeque pit in the back yard.

The was a picturesque setting, one that Norman Rockwell or Thomas Kinkade might have painted. How could such a place mask the type of evil Tyler suspected of Kevin? Looks were often deceiving, though, and Rosaline reminded herself that anything was possible, anywhere.

She knocked on the door, waited, and when no one answered, knocked a second time. Maybe Kevin's wife, Catherine, wouldn't answer. After all, her husband had just died. Who was this stranger at her door? Why would she agree to talk to her? Had something happened to Catherine, too?

Before her dark thoughts spun out of control, the front door opened. A late thirties, early forties, brunette stood at the door. She'd been crying. Her tired, green eyes were filled with so much despair that Rosaline felt guilty for the intrusion. She was thin-framed and wore a grey cardigan over a black dress. She was attractive; Rosaline wondered what she looked like dressed to the nines, in full make-up. Her wedding ring sparkled in the sunlight, highlighting the loss of the person who gave it to her.

"Mrs. Johnstone? I'm Rosaline Maxwell, a former attorney, and former judge. If you're up to it, I'd like to discuss your husband's death. Fill in some blanks."

"I don't need a lawyer," Catherine protested. "I've done nothing wrong. I had nothing to do with Kevin's death. We loved each other very much."

Her reaction surprised Rosaline. Why would Catherine leap to the conclusion she was being investigated? Was it guilt? Was she waiting for someone to charge her with Kevin's murder? Waiting to confess?

Her reaction made Rosaline immediately suspicious and glad she came. Now, she needed a pretense to persuade the widow to share intimate details about her husband, their relationship, and any enemies he might have had.

"I'm not here to offer my services as a lawyer," Rosaline admitted.

"No? Then who are you and why are you here? State your business. I just lost my husband. I'm in mourning," Catherine groused, glaring at Rosaline.

"I'm here to prevent an injustice from occurring. I'm terribly sorry about your husband. I met him for the first time, yesterday. He seemed like a charming man; someone I'd have liked to know better. I'm not sure how much you know about the status of the probe, but the official focus is on Tyler Guthrie as the principal suspect. I know Tyler very well. He's incapable of killing someone and I worry that an innocent man will be punished, and a murderer will continue to walk our streets," Rosaline explained.

"I work as an advocate for those who have been wrongfully convicted and imprisoned. I'm a recognized expert in the field. My goal is to clear Tyler's name before there is any long-term damage to his reputation. At the same time, I hope to unmask the real murderer and bring that person to justice."

Catherine looked confused, not sure what to do. Rosaline didn't blame her. On the one hand, Rosaline might be assisting her husband's murderer. On the other, Rosaline sought to identify and prosecute the real culprit. Catherine's cooperation hinged upon her own opinion of Tyler and whether she believed him capable of offing her husband. Rosaline was desperate to talk to Catherine— she was Rosaline's best lead, someone who might provide answers to important questions.

"We can't bring Kevin back, but I'm sure he'd be concerned about your safety," Rosaline argued. "If the true killer remains at large, that person might come after you and your family. You might be in danger. Your *children* might be in danger. Targeting the wrong man puts *everyone* in danger."

Catherine was silent. Rosaline assumed she was considering the wisdom of her words, still not fully on board. She faced an uncertain future and the possibility that anything she said might be used against her, making her a possible suspect. Like Tyler, though, if Catherine was innocent, she'd want to help identify her husband's killer. Wouldn't she? Identifying a personal benefit from talking might be the best way to convince her to talk.

"Catherine. Please let me help you. I was a lawyer, then a judge for a long time. You dismissed the possibility of needing a lawyer too harshly and too quickly," Rosaline advised. "You are not a professional witness, but I am a professional interrogator. I can help you if you'll let me. Together, perhaps we can find the truth."

Rosaline's words had the opposite of her intended effect. Catherine became more defensive. She crossed her arms over her chest, ready to tell Rosaline to take a hike.

"I understand why you're suspicious," Rosaline continued. "You've done nothing wrong. You're mourning the death of your husband. But when someone is murdered, suspicion always focuses on the person closest to the victim, which includes the spouse. That's just the way the police officers are wired. Expect to be questioned."

Catherine calmed, considering Rosaline's words. Rosaline hoped this was a positive sign.

"Talking things over with me will help prepare you for an official interrogation," Rosaline continued. "I was a judge. I know what questions they will ask. I can help you prepare, and my reputation is solid with law enforcement. I can even assist you when you're questioned. My number one goal is to find the truth and the real killer."

While Catherine mulled over Rosaline's offer, Rosaline rehashed the pitch in her mind—had she made a reasonable case for herself? Was she compelling?

Many years ago, she was skilled at the art of persuasion, but she hadn't tried to convince anyone of anything in a very long time. She awaited Catherine's decision.

"Okay," Catherine decided. "Come on in. I have nothing to hide, and I want this person caught. If you can assist in that endeavor . . ." She held the screen door open and stepped aside to allow Rosaline to enter.

Nothing to hide. Rosaline considered her declaration. *Everyone has something to hide*, her legal experience told her. *Everyone has secrets*. Rosaline willed herself to keep an open mind as she entered the home.

"I'm determined to expose the truth, but I need your help," Rosaline began. "You know the people in Kevin's world, those he got along with, and those he didn't. I need to identify potential suspects. Who were the important players? Do you understand? No one knows a man better than his wife."

"I'm not convinced of that, but I will do anything to help you find out who did this."

Rosaline stopped in the foyer and permitted Catherine to lead her inside the tidy, near-perfect home. It was awash in shades of yellow, white, and grey, which made the house seem cheerful and pleasant. Rosaline loved the décor.

Rosaline was somewhat surprised at the home's condition. Considering Catherine's current circumstances, Rosaline expected a bit of a mess. On the contrary, it was immaculate and meticulously maintained, with inviting vanilla and rose aroma in the air.

"The children are with their grandparents. We're quite alone. I can talk openly," Catherine advised, as she led Rosaline into the living room. Catherine pointed to a white chair and sat down in a matching chair, facing it. Rosaline sat down across from her. A low fire burned in a light grey stone fireplace to their left, creating a sense of warmth and peace.

"Kevin's death is as difficult as it is shocking to all of us who loved him," Catherine began. "I'm still trying to process the fact that he's gone. That's why I sent the kids to my parents. I needed some alone time. They'll be back tomorrow, and we can begin the healing process, together, as a family."

"I'm so sorry for your loss," Rosaline offered. If Catherine was guilty, she was a wonderful actress. If she was innocent, Rosaline imagined how shocked she must be to lose her husband to such horrible violence. Her mind flashed to Kevin's body, lying at the bottom of those stone steps. Rosaline's heart ached for Catherine. "Death under these sudden and tragic circumstances must be horrible for all of you. How are the children holding up?"

"As you can imagine," Catherine sighed. "They're heartbroken. But they are doing their best. As for me, I never thought I'd be a widow at this age. I'm not sure how to mourn, how I'm supposed to behave. I'm doing my best to cope, to not fall apart, for the children."

Catherine drifted away in thought. She appeared lost, which caused Rosaline to question whether she visited too soon after the tragedy. If the woman was suffering, Rosaline was reluctant to contribute to her pain. But something made her suspicious. *Did she exaggerate the family bond?*

"The sudden death of a person we love is never easy," Rosaline began. "I wonder, though. Forgive me if I'm overstepping, but I look around and see all these beautiful family photos. Kevin isn't in any of them. Why is that?"

Catherine steeled. Rosaline's observation caused her to glance around the house, studying the photographs. There were plenty of photos of Catherine with her children, friends, and family, but none included her husband.

"You're quite right," Catherine acquiesced, with little emotion. "I recently removed them—it doesn't mean anything."

"I'm not suggesting it does," Rosaline assured. "But for me to properly investigate Kevin's death, I need to understand everything that's been going on in his life."

"I understand. It will all come out in the inquiry. There's no keeping this under wraps. In truth, things were difficult and tense between my husband and me in the days before his death. We'd been fighting, some of our fights were quite nasty. I wasn't sure the relationship would survive. We were considering a divorce. We even had papers drawn up. Shortly before he died, though, we decided to try to work through our disagreements. Our marriage was worth saving. We loved each other very much. We have a beautiful family and refused to give up on it.

"In fact, in the weeks before his death, things had improved. We began to regain the passion that couples lose in a comfortable long-term relationship. Picture a young couple, falling in love for the first time. Simultaneously, we were working through our differences. I loved him. Our relationship was healing. I had no reason to hurt him, let alone *kill* him."

Catherine's eyes teared, displaying true despair. Rosaline wondered, again, whether her emotions were genuine or whether she belonged in Hollywood. She sensed Catherine was telling the truth or enough of the truth. Her words rung true, genuine. *I don't know her; she might just be a terrific actress.*

Was Catherine lying? Twisting the truth to make herself look less guilty? After all, Kevin was no longer around to contest her version of the truth. Divorces were messy, even more so when kids and assets were involved. Perhaps Catherine feared she might lose custody of valuable assets—might those concerns be a motive for murder? No less than Tyler wanting him gone from the university.

"It must be quite painful for this to occur when you were just rekindling the flame. I'm so sorry. Of course, that's more reason to figure out who committed the evil deed. Kevin deserves justice, as do you and your children.

"If you don't mind, I'd like to start with this: Can you think of anyone who might have a reason to want him dead? I'd like to widen the net, develop a list of suspects, and narrow down the list. Who comes to mind when you consider people who didn't like your husband? Anyone with a motive to kill him?"

"Candidly, yes," Catherine admitted. "Kevin could be a bit of . . . a prick. He was an excellent law professor and teacher. He was charming when he wanted to be—I was the ultimate victim of his charm, at least, at the beginning of our relationship.

"But he tended to ruffle feathers. Kevin had a good news-bad news personality. People either loved or hated him. There was no in-between. I was the exception, I guess. For me, there were both extremes. Sometimes I loved him; sometimes I hated his guts. Recently though, as I said earlier, we were in love mode."

"Understood. Can you give me examples of people who were on the other extreme? The 'I hate Kevin' people?"

"Some students might fall into that category," Catherine opined. "He was a stern, unbending teacher. If students were struggling, Kevin had no problem failing them, crushing their dreams. He would not consider extra credit assignments to boost failing grades. To Kevin, the law was a sacred profession. People who wanted law degrees, wanted to practice law, needed to *earn* the degree and the right to practice. No exceptions.

"We talked about his students quite a bit. He'd tell me about a particular student, and I'd lobby for leniency. He was so rigid, so hard on them. He insisted that judges were also rigid, harsh even, and this was how the students would learn about life in the courtroom. He was unwavering in that regard.

"As you well know, law school is not for the faint of heart. It can be ruthless. People pay a fortune in tuition, work extremely hard. Perhaps they just don't have what it takes. Is it fair to quality students to pass those who should fail? Is it fair to the legal profession? Why spend three hard years in law school only to fail as a lawyer? What was the point? Find another career. That was my Kevin. So, yes, he often received threats from students who failed or were failing his class."

"Threats that might lead to his death—*students*?" She thought back to her years in law school. Students routinely flunked out in the initial semesters, but she couldn't remember or imagine anyone becoming so angry about their dismissal that they would threaten the life of a professor, much less *kill* one. Law school competition was cutthroat and high stakes. She had to concede the possibility that students with dreams of becoming lawyers, who invested their life savings to do so, might have a motive to off someone who crushed those dreams and wasted their money.

"I'm afraid so. Kevin kept meticulous records of all such threats. He gave them to Tyler Guthrie. According to Kevin, Tyler was much less rigid about these issues. He believed students deserved time to acclimate themselves to the rigors of law school. 'Give a kid a break every now and then,' Tyler used to argue. But Kevin refused, which caused a lot of friction between them.

"Kevin had many other complaints. Because of their disagreement on grades, Tyler wouldn't give Kevin the time of day on these other complaints. Kevin was insulted. He thought Tyler had a vendetta against him."

"Both men were professionals. Professionals disagree all the time. Why would this create so much animosity?" Rosaline was confused.

Catherine blanched. "I'm not sure," she responded. "But it was pressing enough for Kevin to consider moving to another university. In fact, he almost left a year ago. Got a job offer, accepted it, and was all set to leave. I was happy for him. A fresh start at a new school was the best solution for both men. Who needed all this grief?

"At the last second, Kevin rescinded his acceptance and decided to stay. I have no idea why. He loved this place, I guess. Perhaps that's what led to his death. Staying at the school. I would not be surprised if your Mr. Guthrie was involved. I would have to respectfully disagree with your assurances that he is innocent."

Rosaline felt wounded. She wanted to defend her friend, but would have to wait for a better time, place, and person. Besides, she pledged to consider all evidence, all points of view, even those she didn't agree with.

"Your fact-finding mission should begin and end with that school," Catherine determined. "Even if Tyler didn't kill him, someone there did. That's where the murder took place and where he received threats. There are plenty of potential suspects who didn't like or even hated my husband. And that's the truth. Tyler, the students, students' parents who wasted their money, other faculty members? In retrospect, I wish he quit when he had the opportunity. I'm convinced he would still be alive . . ." She drifted off, tears welling up in her eyes, heading for a meltdown.

Catherine burst into tears. Rosaline froze, not sure what to do. She wanted to offer reassurance. *I'll bring the bastard to justice.* Instead, she sat speechless. Ultimately, she decided to take her leave, and return another day, when emotions weren't so raw. After Catherine composed herself, she showed Rosaline out of the house.

Rosaline sat in her RV, processing the discussion. She entered the Johnstone home with Tyler as the prime suspect and left the same way. However, she now had a list of new suspects, including the widow. While Catherine made a compelling case for her innocence, she still had a solid motive. *Hell hath no fury, and all that shit.* But when the detectives came calling, Catherine Johnstone would name Tyler Guthrie as the person most likely to have committed the crime. Unless Rosaline unraveled the mystery, Tyler's fate as the principal suspect was sealed.

Rosaline still believed Tyler incapable of committing such a horrific crime. She intended to prove his innocence. With a heavy heart, she started the RV and began her drive toward the school. Perhaps people who loved Tyler and detested Kevin would come forward. Perhaps she could develop and interview additional suspects. But what if Tyler continued to be suspect number one?

Tyler said Kevin Johnstone was a bad person. Instead of investigating potential suspects, she decided to investigate the victim. With whom had Kevin interacted in the days or hours preceding his death? What was the sum and substance of those interactions? Who was angry enough to have a motive? She had to concede that one of those persons was Tyler Guthrie. Would all investigatory trails end at his feet? With all her heart, she prayed that the answer was 'no.'

Chapter Seven

Rosaline returned to campus unsure of her next steps in the probe. Was she cut out for this? Investigators investigate, lawyers litigate, judges judge. Should she leave things to the pros? While not illegal for her to question potential witnesses or suspects, she wanted to do so in an effective manner. Consent to chat was required, of course, but so was a certain expertise. There was an art to convincing people to talk. After two interviews, the principal suspect continued to be Tyler Guthrie.

She gravitated to the library, familiar ground in her life, pulled out her laptop, and inserted the memory stick from Tyler's office. Catherine indicated that Kevin filed multiple complaints against students who threatened him. Rosaline hoped to find records that supported Catherine's allegation and the identity of the complaining students. The president of the school had to have that information stored on his computer.

She scrolled through multiple files. After a detailed search, she found what she was looking for. Tyler had complaint files on four students and three professors. The complaining party for all seven files was Kevin Johnstone. Kevin did not demand discipline or any particular action or penalty, he just wanted to paper the file in case anything occurred in the future.

Like what? Why were these complaints necessary? Why was making a record so important to Kevin? Dying at the hands of a murderer was certainly an important event in Kevin Johnstone's future. Did one of these complaints lead to his death? Did he know he was in danger? If so, why didn't he report the threat or follow up on the complaint?

Rosaline was convinced there was more to the story. If Kevin thought a particular threat was urgent, he would have gone to the authorities. Furthermore, whether Tyler liked Kevin or not, he would not have permitted anyone to threaten bodily harm to one of his professors. He would have dealt with the matter swiftly and authoritatively.

Rosaline decided to leave the library and stroll the campus. Perhaps she might spot a familiar face from Kevin's complaint files. She walked to the crim pro and civil pro lecture halls and professor offices. One office belonged to a professor whose name appeared in Kevin's records. Rosaline knocked on the door. A polite "come in" was heard on the other side of the door. Rosaline opened the door and stepped into the office.

"Hello." Rosaline was greeted with a warm smile by a young woman. Auburn curls fell around her pale cheeks, framing copper eyes. She radiated warmth.

"You're Rosaline Maxwell, aren't you? I recognize you from your lecture yesterday. I'm honored by your visit. I'm Tina

Robinson. As the sign says, I teach criminal law. How may I help you?"

"Do you have a moment to answer a couple of questions?"

"Sure," Tina volunteered. "What's up?"

Rosaline remembered her from the book signing. The young professor was a fan of her work. Perhaps that might work in her favor. Obviously, she was interested in wrongful convictions and punishments. She'd naturally be open-minded to an inquiry designed to prevent a similar injustice.

"I'm here about the Kevin Johnstone situation. I'm conducting my own, private inquiry. I cannot accept the idea that Tyler Guthrie murdered anyone," Rosaline advised.

Tina's face and bubbly demeanor shifted to suspicious and apprehensive. She looked like a suspect in an interrogation room, seeking the exit door. To Rosaline's surprise, though, she didn't shut down the interview.

"Shut the door behind you, please." She looked over Rosaline's shoulder to see if anyone was listening in the outer hallway.

Rosaline shut the door. Tina motioned for Rosaline to have a seat in one of two side chairs that faced her desk. Rosaline sat down.

"As you may know, Tyler Guthrie is a friend; I've known him since our college days. I believe he's incapable of this kind of violence," Rosaline began. "That's why I was invited to lecture."

"I agree, one hundred percent," Tina gushed. "Tyler's not only a good person, he's a very progressive and effective leader. The university has prospered under his leadership. But when you showed up asking about Kevin, I figured it had something to do with Tyler. There have been rumors that Tyler was brought in for questioning. It's impossible for me to believe that he had anything to do with Kevin's death."

"I hate to be the bearer of bad news, Tina, may I call you Tina?"

"You may, indeed. What's the bad news?"

"Tyler hasn't only been questioned," Rosaline corrected. "He's behind bars, being held on suspicion of murder. Investigators think he did it."

"No way!" Tina gasped. "What evidence do they have? Tyler? Ridiculous!"

"I know, and you know. Not *our* Tyler," Rosaline reasoned. "But investigators are far more objective. They don't know him, and, so far, the evidence seems to support their suspicions. I fear they've found their suspect and won't look further. That's why I've started to conduct my own private review of the evidence. So far, all my own sleuthing has revealed is that Tyler clearly didn't like Kevin."

"That's probably true. Most of us detested Kevin. But it's a stretch to say that disliking someone, even intensely, is a motive to *kill* him. I know the criminal mind. I teach criminal law. Taking a life requires a certain mindset and a compelling motive. Tyler Guthrie has neither. I don't want to trash the dead, but if disliking

Kevin Johnstone is a motive for murder, put my name down and the names of almost every student and professor on this campus!"

"I only met him yesterday, but I understand that some people found Kevin to be a particularly smooth and charming man. Most see through his charming mask and see a very dark soul.

"I understand that you had a run-in with Kevin and some sort of complaint was filed. Might you elaborate?"

Tina blushed. "I have had my issues with him," she conceded. "As have many others. In the case of Kevin Johnstone, almost everyone on campus is a suspect. For the record, Ms. Maxwell . . ."

"Please, call me 'Rosaline.'"

"For the record, Rosaline, I did not kill Kevin Johnstone. That's how I know that having a disagreement with a disagreeable, complaint-filing idiot is not necessarily a motive for murder." Tina scowled, looked away, paused, and collected herself. When she spoke again, her voice was calmer, softer.

"Frankly, Rosaline, he was quite an asshole, bottom line. He has aggressively flirted with attractive female students and professors since the day I arrived on campus. Some found him charming. I found him repulsive and rejected his advances. As for me, even if I had been interested in him, which I was *not*, he had a wife and two kids. I would never be 'the other woman' in a love triangle with a married man. It takes a certain type of woman to help break up a family.

"Kevin is not someone who takes kindly to rejection. He filed a bogus complaint about me to Tyler. He accused *me* of coming on to *him*! But Tyler believed me over Kevin—apparently, I was not his first victim. Tyler deposited the complaint in the proverbial round file. There was no hearing or discipline, which would have looked horrible on my record. After it happened, I kept my eye on Kevin, watched him from a distance, if you know what I mean. And I was shocked by the things I saw."

"Like what?"

"Deceitful stuff, he was a scumbag," Tina charged. "He flirted with many attractive and even some unattractive female professors, many of whom were married. I can't substantiate this, but there were rumors he offered certain female students elevated grades in exchange for sexual favors. He was a womanizer and a cheater—no one, and I mean *no one* liked Kevin Johnstone."

"Why not fire the guy?"

"Tenure would be my guess. To overcome tenure, the allegations had to be conclusively proven. Most of the complaints were of the 'he said-she said' variety. I'm convinced that's why Kevin filed so many. He correctly determined that the best defense is an aggressive offense. Tyler is not one to put up with such behavior, but tenure tied his hands. He needed concrete proof. Kevin was a smart guy, a lawyer's lawyer, someone who never put anything in writing unless it benefitted him, said or did anything in front of a witness. There was insufficient proof to overcome his tenure status.

"Besides, as you mentioned, Kevin could be quite charming when he needed to be. The board of directors, for instance, *loved* Kevin. That made Tyler's job even more difficult. If he wanted to expel Kevin, he'd have to make a compelling, almost airtight case, and convince the board to see the light. Kevin was virtually untouchable to those in power around here."

Tina paused, weighing her next comment. Rosaline leaned forward, infringing on Tina's space. In Rosaline's experience, reluctant words, those uttered after careful thought, were the most important.

"There are rumors he blackmailed people." Tina looked left, then right, as if someone might be listening. "These were only rumors, I must emphasize that fact. Kevin is dead; I don't want to spread my own rumors, especially about someone who is not here to defend himself. But there are lots of these floating around. They've been around for a long time and have never died down— more prevalent on the day he died, than ever before. In my opinion, Kevin's ability to find dirt on anyone who might harm him is what has always enabled him to survive in what can only be described as a hostile environment . . . of his own making, of course."

Rosaline considered Tina's bold allegations. They made perfect sense. Blackmail could have prevented people from making complaints or following up on complaints made. It would also explain why there were more complaints filed by Kevin than against him, why he held his position as a professor until the day he died, and why Tyler Guthrie was so frustrated.

"Did Kevin blackmail you?" Rosaline challenged.

Tina blanched. She avoided eye contact. Kevin had something on her and used it to prevent her from complaining about him. She was forthcoming about his repugnant behavior because he was dead, hence she was safe. But, would someone kill for a similar reason?

She denied it, however. "Kevin Johnstone never blackmailed me because there is nothing to blackmail me about. Besides, these are just rumors. I have no idea if Kevin blackmailed *anyone*."

Rosaline nodded. "Understood."

But Rosaline was now convinced that Kevin *had* blackmailed people. Tina Robinson was likely one of those people. How many blackmail victims were out there? The case was becoming more complicated. Kevin had made lots of enemies and, as such, created lots of suspects and plenty of reasons to believe someone else, besides Tyler, may have killed Kevin.

Tina was forthcoming, which Rosaline appreciated. It made her story more believable, even if she withheld the blackmail details. Would other blackmail victims be as cooperative? Kevin was dead; that would help, but would they prefer to stay silent? Avoid becoming involved? Time would tell.

"This was quite helpful—I really appreciate your candor," Rosaline lauded. "I know Tyler didn't do this and I intend to do everything in my power to make sure the person who did is brought to justice. Here's my card. It has my cell phone. Call me if you think of anything else."

"I will. Tyler is lucky to have you in his corner," Tina remarked. "I wish you every success. Glad you stopped by. It was cathartic to talk freely about Kevin."

"I'm glad you feel that way. Any suggestions on who I should visit next? Does anyone stand out in the crowd?"

"Not really. There are plenty of Kevin-haters, but none that I can fathom murdering him. Since I share the sentiment and know I didn't do it, it would be disingenuous to point the finger at someone else. Besides, they are easy to find on this campus. Look for anyone who had routine contact with Kevin Johnstone. They are as likely as me to dislike this very dislikeable man, but not likely to do the evil deed."

"Got it," Rosaline understood, deciding to leave things alone. She would move onto the next suspect.

Tina was correct. There was a long list of potential suspects. Rosaline talked to many. It was now clear that Kevin was a well-known womanizer and serial cheater, someone who resorted to unsavory means to maintain his prestigious position on campus. He was a master manipulator whose final act landed him in the morgue.

It was a fruitful day. Tyler was innocent, and she had now developed numerous alternative suspects, the very definition of reasonable doubt. She would present these discoveries to Detective Remer and use them to arrange bail for her friend. Together, they would unravel the mystery of Kevin Johnstone's untimely death.

Chapter Eight

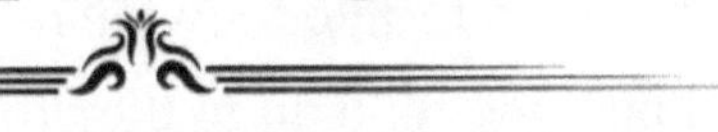

After a long day, Rosaline wrapped up her on-campus interviews. Rather than check in with Remer, she decided to drive home. Besides, he wouldn't be in his office at this hour and no one at the station would be familiar enough with the case to take anything she offered seriously. She was concerned nothing would be passed down. She'd go to the station in the morning. For now, her mission was to head home for some much needed sleep.

After an uneventful drive home, Rosaline made herself a nightcap, slugged it down, took a shower, donned a pair of jogging shorts and a tee shirt, and crawled into bed. She thought she'd be asleep the moment her head hit the pillow. But sleep was difficult to come by. She lay in bed, tossing and turning, thinking of Tyler in a cold jail cell. This had to be hard on him. *He must be suffering.* He was a fragile human being, and these were difficult circumstances. She wanted desperately to rescue him. Hopefully, her morning meeting with Detective Remer would result in a bail hearing and the posting of reasonable bail.

The following morning, on less than three hours of restless sleep, Rosaline Maxwell walked into Harbor Springs headquarters. She never expected to investigate every lead on her own. Her strategy was to give Remer and his crew something to think about, alternative suspects to interview, and alternative leads to follow. Then, she'd punt the football to the professionals and let them run with it. They had unlimited resources and manpower; she did not. If they took her evidence seriously, they would do a much better job.

She approached the sergeant's desk and asked for Remer. He'd be in shortly, the desk sergeant advised. He invited her to take a seat in a small waiting area. As she waited, her thoughts turned to Tyler. *Imagine his relief when I walk him out of that cell!* Food was notoriously lousy in prison. She decided to take him for breakfast, the minute he walked out of the prison complex.

Afterward, they'd go to his house and go over her notes, plot strategy, perhaps allow him to vent his uncomfortable emotions. They'd brainstorm new ideas, alternate theories, suspects, and try to uncover, at the very least, reasonable doubt. Or, perhaps, they'd hit a home run and come up with the actual killer.

Perhaps they wouldn't talk about the case, at least, not at first. She'd make sure he was settled, comfortable, ready to decompress. She'd simply be a friend indeed in Tyler's time of need. There would be plenty of time to search for the truth.

Whatever Tyler's pleasure, she would be there for him and support his wishes, in whatever capacity he needed. When it was over, after he was fully exonerated, Rosaline would return to the book tour and Tyler would go back to his day job, as the world's greatest school president. *Everything will return to normal . . . won't it?*

Hope filled her heart as she waited for Remer. She was proud of her work, grateful she'd stayed long enough to do it. It was time to turn things over to the pros. Minutes turned into a half-hour, then an hour, as she waited, anxious to unload all she discovered.

Almost an hour-and-a-half after she entered the station, Remer walked through the door. Rosaline rose and called out to him. He turned and offered a friendly smile with what Rosaline noted was a bit of tension behind it.

"Nice to see you again, Rosaline" he chirped. "What brings you here this morning?"

"I have some important information about the Johnstone case. I believe you will find it interesting."

Rosaline was heartened by the fact that Remer didn't blow her off. Yes, Tyler was his principal suspect, but that didn't blind him to alternatives. Tyler had not been formally charged. Perhaps there was a remote chance to persuade the obstinate detective to consider other suspects or theories.

"Let's chat in my executive office," he deadpanned. "It's too chaotic to think out here in the pit."

Remer led Rosaline into a cramped office in the bowels of the station. His desk was littered with paperwork. His wall was dotted with awards for longevity, valor, and courage. This was the office of a stressed, overworked, civil servant. In contrast, Tyler's desk was large, executive style, warm and inviting, designed to entice money out of wealthy donors and alumni.

Remer's office was in such disarray that Rosaline worried he'd miss important tips about the case or misplace valuable evidence. Did he have ample time to investigate? Would he thoroughly consider and examine all possibilities? What choice did she have other than to allow him to do his job?

"Have a seat," he offered, motioning to a chair opposite his desk. "I'm guessing you're here about the recent developments in the case."

"Developments?" Rosaline queried, as she sat.

Remer collapsed into his chair, looking as though he regretted opening his mouth. "You're a former circuit court judge," he noted. "I assumed you had ways of staying in the loop since the case involves a friend."

"I'm extremely interested and quite invested, too, but no, I don't have some magic wand I can wave to obtain inside information. Please tell me, what developments?" Rosaline all but demanded.

Remer averted his eyes, looked out a very narrow window, almost too dirty to see through. When his eyes returned to meet hers, he looked tired, tired of asking questions, of private citizens trying to act like cops, and of people questioning his judgment and authority. Remer looked ready to move on to other cases. Rosaline was terrified.

"I understand you've been sticking your nose in our business, talking to potential witnesses, visiting family members without invitations. You're wasting your time, lady. Tyler Guthrie is guilty as hell. That's that, case over."

Rosaline shook her head. "I vehemently disagree," she insisted. "Quite the contrary. In only one day on the case, I've discovered multiple people who hated the victim and had solid motives to kill Johnstone. He was not a popular guy—apparently, he was kind of a jerk. He was universally detested by almost everyone.

"If you're going to arrest Tyler Guthrie for disliking Kevin Johnstone, put Tyler in line behind a thousand teachers, administrators, students, and relatives. Kevin thrived on conflict, with just about *everyone*.

"I hate to disparage the dead, but Kevin was manipulative, a liar, a serial womanizer, an adulterer, and a blackmailer. Many people hated him, which is the ticket to reasonable doubt for Tyler Guthrie. Whatever motive he may have had to kill Kevin, is no stronger than any of the others' motives.

"Furthermore, he is needed to assist in his own defense. He's not a danger to society—he has a spotless record and the proofs, in this case, are faulty. His pen was found at the scene, but he is always out and about on school grounds. There are no eyewitnesses, no forensics linking Tyler to the scene, and, again, no unique motive. It's time to release him on his own recognizance. Give Tyler and I a chance to prove his innocence. Or, better yet, do your job. Investigate the case and the other suspects, thoroughly, instead of pinning the crime on the easiest scapegoat."

Rosaline remained calm through her mini-tirade. She was passionate and firm, but above all, lucid and believable. She did not want to allow her emotions to cloud her judgment. She strived to appear unbiased. However, she would not stand aside and allow lazy cops to railroad an innocent man.

"Are you quite finished?" Remer snickered. "Another amateur sleuth who thinks she can do my job better than me. If I had a nickel for every . . ." He stopped in his tracks, assessing Rosaline.

"I must confess that none of them were former judges with years of experience. That counts for something in my book."

"Why Detective Remer, was that a . . . *compliment*?" Rosaline chuckled.

"Look, Rosaline. I know you and Guthrie have history. I know you believe he's innocent. I may even decide to investigate your list of suspects." He leaned back in the old chair. It creaked and moaned. Rosaline feared the tension springs might snap and send the man to the floor.

"I am aware that Kevin had a few enemies. We can talk to these people, dive into their dealings with Kevin and their whereabouts at the time of his death. But Tyler Guthrie stays in lock-up. We've got more on him than a grudge and a pen."

"Really?" Rosaline snipped, leaning into Remer, looking him in the eye. "I'd love to hear your evidence. What smoking gun do you have to justify keeping Tyler Guthrie in lock-up?"

"As long as you asked so nicely, and because we will have to show probable cause for the arrest, try this on for size: You mentioned that Kevin was a blackmailer, right? We found evidence that he was, indeed, blackmailing someone. Blackmail is a crime in this state, Rosaline. I don't have to tell you that. But it does not carry the death penalty, and even if it did, we law enforcement types do not condone vigilante justice. Can we agree on that?"

"Of course," Rosaline conceded.

"And we would also agree that nothing Johnstone did justifies a sentence of death. As such, it is important to seek justice for him," Remer noted.

"No argument from me on that score," Rosaline concurred. "Even his multiple offenses did not deserve a death sentence. There are many bad people in this world, and they live long unpleasant lives. No one should die for being a lousy person. I'd like to help you solve this case if you'll let me. Blackmail is a notable motive."

"I'm glad you acknowledge that," Remer continued. "Because the person Kevin Johnstone was blackmailing was none other than Tyler Guthrie." The cop dropped the bombshell.

Rosaline's heart sank. She felt nauseous. What did Kevin possibly know and use to blackmail Tyler?

"H-how?" she stammered. "Tyler has no deep, dark secrets. I've known him for years. There's nothing worth blackmailing him over. Tyler is the finest man I know. You must be mistaken."

"Unfortunately, we're not," Remer insisted. "We have solid evidence that Kevin was blackmailing Tyler. You don't know Tyler as well as you think you do. It is you who is mistaken. You are so blinded by loyalty, you're unable to see Tyler for who and what he really is."

"I've done my due diligence, Detective Remer," she contended. "There are multiple suspects, multiple possibilities, and Tyler Guthrie is not guilty of this crime, blackmail or not. And, as I indicated, Johnstone is a serial blackmailer. If you know he's blackmailed one person, is it really a stretch to assume and investigate the fact that he's blackmailed others? If you do investigate, and he has committed multiple acts of blackmail, there is reasonable doubt with multiple alternative suspects."

Remer sighed as he studied her. "I don't go divulging State's evidence to just anyone before it's introduced at trial or sentencing, but since you're a former judge and won't let this go, here's the straight scoop:

"Tyler was involved in an academic cheating scandal. He was paid huge sums of money by the rich and famous to help students of wealthy donors pass classes. He gathered curriculum from professors, including test answers, and provided them to students whose parents paid to obtain them.

"He also changed grades in the database, if necessary, to suit wealthy benefactors and their children. This is an open case, and we are tracking down leads to others who may be involved, but Tyler Guthrie is a principal co-conspirator. He may be the kingpin in the whole operation.

"Kevin discovered the scandal, obtained secret files, and assembled documents to prove Tyler's involvement, including a video of Tyler engaged in long conversations with students involved in the scandal. Several of these students may become whistleblowers. Johnstone kept a detailed, indexed file on the scandal and your friend Tyler. And then, as bad guys are prone to do, instead of turning Guthrie over to the feds, he decided to blackmail the man. Johnstone had a 'come to Jesus' moment and decided to come forward, too little, too late. Tyler killed him to shut him up and keep him from involving the feds. The timing is too coincidental to ignore."

Rosaline was shocked. The thought of Tyler Guthrie being part of an academic scandal was too ridiculous to fathom. He was a passionate educator. He wanted students to work hard, *earn* their success, learn, grow, and become responsible members of society. In fact, Tyler was directly responsible for thousands of students who did just that. A cheating scandal was the antithesis of what Tyler Guthrie was all about. He would never do that—it violated his moral code. Every fiber in Rosaline's being told her that Remer was mistaken. If the cop had solid evidence, it had to be manufactured, probably by Kevin.

Remer continued. "I know it's difficult to come to terms with, but some of the worst people wear the best masks . . ."

"Not possible," Rosaline insisted. "Tyler didn't do it. It makes no sense. The evidence against Tyler must be fabricated and manufactured. Who would have a motive to do that? Kevin Johnstone, that's who! Have you figured out why Kevin needed to blackmail Tyler? What was Kevin hiding?"

"We're not sure yet but . . ."

"My very cursory probe has revealed that Kevin Johnstone was an evil, unsavory character, with questionable morals and ethics. If anyone would be involved in a grade-fixing scandal, it was Kevin. Have you spoken to the accused students? What do they have to say? Have you put the documents through forensic analysis?"

"No one is going to say anything until immunity and plea deals are worked out. As I indicated, this is an ongoing investigation. If the documents are forged, I'm sure our experts will discover that and my attitude toward your friend Tyler might change. As of this moment, Kevin is reaching out to us, through his documents, from the grave. It's eerie, no?"

"*That's* your evidence? The files of a morally and ethically bankrupt professor who thought he was about to be canned? Were you aware of Tyler's file on Kevin, Detective Remer? Did you investigate *that*? Your so-called document trail is a sham. I'll bet my pension on that," Rosaline growled.

"They don't prove anything but what a smart, manipulative criminal Kevin Johnstone was. He had secrets, feared discovery and termination, and figured out a scheme to make it all go away. Have you investigated whether Kevin used his phony documents to extort others? If he did, wouldn't they have motives like Tyler's? Who else did Kevin target? He was willing to blackmail, why not throw a blackmail party and threaten the whole group?

Someone cracked under Kevin's pressure and it sure as hell wasn't Tyler Guthrie. In fact, I challenge you. Let's go over to the jail and run this by Tyler. Let's just ask him who took money from wealthy parents and who blackmailed whom. Are you game?

"Kevin may have scared someone into killing him. But you have too many alternate possibilities to focus on only one. How about extorting his wife by using valuable assets, child custody, or both? How about the women he was having affairs with? How about others involved in the frame on Tyler Guthrie? Many had reason to hate Kevin, just as many had reason to kill him.

"I don't expect a declaration of Tyler's innocence, but I do expect a thorough study of all related matters and reasonable bail for Tyler while you sort this out. I've heard your bombshell evidence, and it isn't enough to hold him, Detective.

"I believe you are good police. I believe you will eventually find the truth. Put a tether on him, if you must, but this innocent man should not spend one more minute in prison."

"Tyler Guthrie is not innocent," Remer snapped. "And I am not just good, lady, I'm *very* good. I don't appreciate what you're insinuating. We have plenty of evidence to hold your buddy—we are not letting him go. One of these days you will realize Guthrie is not the man you thought he was. He has dark secrets and those secrets led him to committing the crime."

"I don't believe that for a second. You've jumped to conclusions. You must charge him or release him. If you charge him, I'm going to recommend a probable cause hearing. If a local judge hears the evidence I just heard, a bunch of conjecture and speculation without a single *live* witness, he or she will release Tyler. It's not even a close question."

"We'll charge him when we're required to. This conversation is over—I have other cases. Knock yourself out on that probable cause hearing. I know the local judges far better than you do and I am quite confident that Tyler Guthrie, a threat to society, will remain in prison until he is convicted of murder, fraud, and conspiracy. Have a lovely day." He stood, pointed to the door, waited for her to exit, then sat down and picked up a file.

Rosaline stormed out of the station, mad as hell. Remer was not the man she thought. His query thus far was cursory at best and a sham at worst. Any mediocre defense attorney would poke so many holes in this so-called *evidence*, Rosaline could drive a proverbial truck through it. But the idiot gumshoes had made up their minds. They would not search for the truth. *Their* truth was all that mattered and Tyler Guthrie, according to *their* truth, was a cold-blooded killer. It was now up to Rosaline to prove his innocence, beyond a reasonable doubt. Otherwise, Tyler Guthrie would spend the rest of his life in prison.

Chapter Nine

After her stressful encounter with the detective, Rosaline was even more determined to spring Tyler from that horrible prison. He had an attorney, but the guy had a busy practice, multiple deadbeat clients, and an unwillingness to spend the money to retain the quality investigators necessary to expose the truth. Rosaline was on her own. Like Tyler's lawyer, she lacked the resources to hunt down the many potential suspects. Unlike Tyler's lawyer, she had no clients and plenty of time on her hands. She had to be a smart investigator. She would research possibilities and narrow the search to those most likely to commit a violent crime. However, her inexperience continued to haunt her. *Where do I begin? How do I proceed?*

She stopped at a local diner and ordered the breakfast special, eggs, potatoes, toast, and coffee. As she downed her meal, she studied Kevin's files on her laptop. With new evidence of a scandal, she tried to look for potential students and parents who might be involved. Most of what she found was Tyler's discovery and notes about Kevin's suspicious behavior, nothing the other way around. After all, these were Tyler's files, not Kevin's. She needed to see *Kevin's* files. She made a note to talk to Tyler's lawyer about appropriate discovery requests when the time came. She was exhausted and frustrated, about to give up when a note popped up.

Kevin almost resigned to take a position at another school. Would have solved everything, been a relief. I threatened to fire him based on his morals clause and his immoral behavior, and it almost worked. He was about to take the job. What stopped him? Who saved the day? He suspects I'm on to him. Why would he want to stay? I've got solid evidence he's having an affair, but less solid evidence that the affair is with a student. Unfortunately, rumor and innuendo are not enough proof to fire the guy. If he remains on campus, people will be in danger. I must protect my students from this predator. I must find a way to be rid of him.

The note cut both ways. While damning for Tyler, it was damning for Kevin, too. Apparently, this controversy had been percolating for a long time. If Tyler wanted to literally terminate Kevin, why now, after sitting for so long on the information? It made no sense. Remer's crew would consider it a damning piece of evidence. The note also identified a new and interesting suspect. Who was this student, literally in bed with Kevin? How could Rosaline obtain her identity? Was Kevin blackmailing the student or was she blackmailing Kevin? Was she also involved in the grade-fixing scandal? All were solid motives for murder, but how would Rosaline find her?

Rosaline combed Tyler's list of Kevin's students at the time the note was written. She discovered that the note was written during the current term. Thus, the sexual partner, if she existed, was among Kevin's current students. She immediately eliminated all male students, which left 50 potential female students.

She decided to narrow down the list by randomly asking students and professors about rumors of an affair between Professor Johnstone and a student. Perhaps someone heard a name. Perhaps she'd hit the jackpot and some young lady would confess. *Dream on, Rosaline.* She drove home feeling helpless and frustrated. The clock was ticking, Tyler would soon be formally charged, and she still had no concrete solutions.

She willed herself to be patient. Desperate people do desperate things, and she did not want to miss something because she rushed the process. In fact, as she opened her front door, she almost missed the note that fell onto the porch.

Rosaline bent over and secured the folded piece of paper. She glanced around to see if the person who left it was still somewhere in the vicinity. No one around, everything was quiet, she saw no evidence of stranger danger. She chuckled to herself about not feeling any sense of impending doom. Had her senses gone haywire or was there no impending doom?

Just to be sure, she ducked inside, shut and locked the door. She inspected the house and checked all doors and windows. When she was sure that no one was watching, she unfolded and examined the note.

You don't know me. It is worthless to try to discover my identity, you will be wasting your time. I'm someone who is interested in this case. I have pressing concerns about the cops and suspicions about who the perpetrator might be. I have a potential suspect and motive. Enough to think a particular someone may be involved. Tyler Guthrie is a kind man. I doubt he's capable of this type of brutality.

I suggest you consider Lindsey Parker, a student at the university, rumored to be having an affair with Professor Johnstone. This affair, according to rumors, has been ongoing for at least a year. They were spotted flirting outside the classroom and often engaged in intimate conversations. There was something improper going on.

I do not know whether Lindsey was involved in or knows anything about Kevin's death. If they were having an affair, Lindsey, a jealous lover, Johnstone's wife, some woman's husband, or all of the above, might have had something to do with his death. Just something to jumpstart your private inquiry. Best of luck. Rosaline re-read the note multiple times. She wanted to be certain she missed nothing. She now had a solid lead. Someone to investigate besides Tyler and Catherine. No solid proof, but an alternate direction and shortcut to a suspect. Someone to question.

Is it a trap? She considered that possibility. Perhaps she was being sent on a wild goose chase by the perp. After all, she was the only person investigating alternative suspects. Remer and his flatfoot cronies were singularly focused on Tyler Guthrie. This might be a clever diversion.

Even if it was a diversion, Rosaline postulated that if she connected whoever wrote this to Lindsey, she might find the killer.

The best and most obvious strategy moving forward was to confront and interview Lindsey Parker.

However, the thought of questioning the young woman about an unsubstantiated affair with a married man made her uncomfortable. Even the note writer admitted that the affair was no more than a rumor. 'Something was going on' was the best the note writer could say. *How do I approach a woman I hardly know and ask: "Were you sleeping with Kevin Johnstone?"* Rosaline didn't want to accuse anyone of anything.

However, this was her first solid lead pointing away from Tyler, and she was determined to follow it up. She decided to do some research on Lindsey Parker. She pulled out her laptop and connected to the Internet.

She entered the school name and Lindsey Parker as search terms. Lindsey's name popped up as an active student and a journalist for the school newspaper. She was also involved in a few of the school's charity projects. A recent photo was posted on her active student page.

The photo was what caused Rosaline's antenna to rise— Rosaline recognized the young woman in the photo. Staring back at her on the computer screen was the same 'Lindsey' who she met at her book signing, the young woman was so enthralled with Rosaline's work. Rosaline was intrigued by the coincidence and hoped it would help make Lindsey more open to a future conversation. They had already established a friendly connection.

The two women had Tyler in common. The question going forward, of course, was whether Lindsey was 'pro-Tyler' or 'anti-Tyler.' As a student at the school, she had to have interacted with its president from time to time. Were those interactions positive or negative? Perhaps they formed a connection that might incentivize her to help clear Tyler's name. Recalling Lindsey's bubbly personality, Rosaline was upbeat for the first time since agreeing to look into the case. Compliments of the mystery note writer, she had her first promising lead. She headed back to campus to find Lindsey Parker.

Rosaline arrived at the school and went straight to the registrar's office. She explained that she was a former judge who was privately investigating Professor Johnstone's death. The desk clerk took her name and went into the back office. She returned, shaking her head, indicating that a student's personal information was private and releasable only pursuant to a signed authorization from the student or via a court-issued subpoena. As was becoming the norm for this case, Rosaline would have to do things the hard way.

She roamed the campus and began asking random students about Lindsey and where she might be found at this time of day. Some ignored her completely, others gave her somewhat of a cold shoulder, still others eyed her suspiciously and refused to help. Identifying herself as a former judge seemed to make matters worse, not better, so she stopped introducing herself that way. After a long day, she struck pay dirt.

"I recognize you," a young woman responded to Rosaline's inquiry. "You're the writer who gave that wonderful lecture." She was an attractive young lady whose auburn hair fell in front of dark, honey eyes. She seemed eager to assist Rosaline.

"I'm Lindsey's roommate, Raven Conroy. Lindsey can't stop raving about you. She loves your work, obsessively reads your book, and can't wait for the next one. She's also quite passionate about wrongful or unfair incarcerations, and we've had multiple discussions about these issues. She's been talking about changing her major and using her studies to assist or improve the lives of disadvantaged people. I love her enthusiasm—it's very contagious.

"She was so pleased to have met you, still raves about the experience. I'm sure she would be happy to hear from you again. She has no classes this afternoon—she usually goes back to our room to study. I'll walk you over to the dorm now."

Raven led Rosaline through the maze that was the college campus. Rosaline was pumped to be making progress in her probe. They passed the infamous outdoor staircase where Kevin Johnstone took his final steps. After a brisk walk about campus, they arrived at a crowded dormitory. She endured curious glares from students who were unaccustomed to seeing a strange middle-aged woman on campus. Was she someone's mother?

Raven was completely oblivious to the attention they were attracting, as she walked to the end of the hall. She opened her room's door, revealing a tastefully decorated habitat, with gold and black furniture, art on the walls, and books filling every available flat surface on a three-column bookcase.

Lindsey laid on her bed, headphones on, engrossed in a textbook, taking notes on a yellow legal pad. She glanced up as Raven walked in, saw Rosaline, and ripped off her headphones.

"Judge Maxwell!" Lindsey exclaimed, in a breathy tone. "It's so nice to see you! What are you doing here?"

"I'm so sorry to pull you away from your studies," Rosaline began. "But I have something important to discuss with you. Do you have a few minutes to talk?"

"For you? Of course, I do!" She blushed at the prospect of another conversation with her idol. She glanced at Raven. "In private or . . ."

"Whatever makes you more comfortable, my dear." Rosaline preferred to chat privately—these were personal issues and questions about a possible illicit affair, and she did not want to ask them in front of Lindsey's roommate. However, she also saw value in having Raven stay in the room, the place where Lindsey probably was the most comfortable, anything to facilitate open and fruitful conversation. Raven sensed the need for privacy and bailed Rosaline out.

"I have to head to class anyway," Raven chirped. "I'll give you two some privacy. Catch you later. Lindsey. Glad to meet you, Judge Maxwell."

"And you, as well. Thanks for helping me out."

"No prob."

Raven picked up her class books, walked out with a wave, and shut the door. As Rosaline gazed at Lindsey, it stuck her how sensitive a topic this was and how young and naïve Lindsey seemed. Though technically an adult, to an older woman, a college student was no more than a kid.

Consensual or not, the thought of a middle-aged professor engaging in sexual relations with a barely twenty-something student disgusted Rosaline. Even if Lindsay agreed to an affair, the power dynamic in favor of the professor made the relationship less than consensual. Rosaline preferred to see the good in people. Perhaps she was barking up the wrong tree. Perhaps the rumored affair never happened.

She harkened back to Tyler and his comments about Johnstone. He suspected Kevin was harming and blackmailing students. She knew and believed in Tyler. Would he levy such outrageous accusations or charges if they weren't true? Tyler Guthrie wouldn't not do that. Would he?

"Please have a seat," Lindsey offered, interrupting Rosaline's thoughts. The young student pulled out a desk chair. "Not the fanciest or most comfortable accommodations, but . . ."

"It's lovely," Rosaline assured her as she sat in the chair. Lindsey sat back down on her bed.

Rosaline glanced around the room. Fairy lights added to its charm, creating a welcoming and cozy environment. "You've done a wonderful job decorating this space. Most dorm rooms are dumps, a bed, a desk, and a mess. It was a long time ago, but that's what my room looked like."

"Raven and I are faux interior decorators. We tried to make the most of the space. We spend a lot of time in our room, so we attempted to create a pleasing environment for study."

"Well, you did a magnificent job. You know that your education and college experience are game-changers," Rosaline noted. "You're an enthusiastic student—I'll bet you enjoy making your professors happy."

"Sure. Pleasing the profs is what college is all about. College grades can make or break a career. Plus, you need their recommendation letters, insider knowledge, real-world connections, that sort of thing," Lindsey explained.

"Some of my classmates have family businesses or corporate connections. My folks have none of that. I'm completely on my own. That makes professors and administrators even more important.

"My folks never went to college. It was a big reason why they wanted me to go and worked so hard to make it happen. They didn't have much money. My dad used to tell me that education was the ticket to success. I took that to heart. Hopefully, I can prove that he was correct. I want to make him proud."

Rosaline was surprised how immediately forthcoming Lindsey was. She had just met the young student, yet the girl was sharing intimate aspects of her personal life, perhaps, seeking Rosaline's approval. Her willingness to openly engage would probably make it easy for Rosaline to obtain the information she sought. Yet, she felt a tinge of guilt, uneasiness, perhaps sadness for Lindsey. If Johnstone *did* have an affair with Lindsey, he weaponized her need for validation, acceptance, and achievement beyond the level of her parents. The approval of authority figures in her life was clearly something she craved.

"I had a similar experience," Rosaline confided. "My parents weren't wealthy, quite the contrary, in fact. I had a job all the way through college and law school. Sometimes, I ate at the food banks. But I graduated with honors, got some scholarship money that helped me finish law school, and here I am.

"I was able to help my parents out, financially, even though they resisted. It was very gratifying— improving your own station in life can be beneficial to those you love. It was a huge motivator for me. I'm so impressed that you've come this far on your own. You should be quite proud of yourself."

Lindsey blushed. "High praise coming from someone as accomplished as you. I *have* worked very hard."

"I do wonder, though, if one of your teachers might have tried to take advantage of your need for approval. That's the reason I wanted to talk to you," Rosaline postulated. Her eyes were trained on Lindsey's face, looking for her reaction. "Some people sense vulnerability, and prey on it."

"I'm not sure what you mean," Lindsey seemed confused.

"You've indicated how important professors are when you finish college. Are there any with whom you've developed personal relationships?"

"Personal relationships . . . I guess I'm close to a lot of my professors. I try to build solid relationships with all professors and administrators. None have taken advantage. Everyone here has been wonderful. Again, I'm not sure what you mean."

"What was your relationship with Professor Johnstone?" Rosaline pounced. Lindsey blushed and diverted her eyes. Rosaline suspected she was heading in the right direction.

"Kevin?" Lindsey blushed. Rosaline nodded. "We had a solid relationship, not that he ever took advantage. No bad blood or anything—I considered him a mentor. I learned a lot from Professor Johnstone. I was incredibly sad to hear about his passing."

Lindsey said all the right words, but they did not exactly ring true—she looked terribly uncomfortable, and tears welled in her eyes. She seemed embarrassed to be tearful and quickly wiped them away. "Professor Johnstone's death was, indeed, a tragedy," Rosaline agreed. "How did you take the news? Was his death more personal for you than your fellow students?"

"Again, I'm not sure what you mean."

"I'm actually investigating the incident. As you may know, your school president has been charged with killing Professor Johnstone. I know, for a fact, that he is innocent. They've arrested the wrong person. I've been beating around the bush here, and I am just going to come out and ask what I came to ask. According to my research and various rumors around campus, you've been having an affair with Professor Johnstone. I don't want to offend you, but as an investigator, I must follow the leads and the evidence. So . . . were you . . . having an affair?"

Lindsey froze—Rosaline awaited her response.

Chapter Ten

"I never heard any rumors. And, besides, absolutely not—there was no improper relationship. Kevin and I shared a normal, completely platonic, student/teacher dynamic." Lindsey responded, after a moment of shocked silence. "I have tremendous respect for you, but I resent what you're implying. Where are you hearing these so-called rumors?"

"My source is quite reliable," Rosaline persisted. "I'm not here to judge. I'm here to try to clear an innocent man's name. No one believes you had anything to do with Kevin's death. However, if you and Kevin did have an affair, that would mean you knew him better than most around here. I'm trying to solve his murder. If he was having an affair, and his wife found out, she would be a potential suspect. When I talked with her, she was less than forthcoming, hiding something important. I'm not seeing the full picture, which is impeding my work to exonerate Tyler. People in Kevin's immediate orbit can provide more context and detail about potential suspects. Who had a reason to want him dead?"

"Catherine's only concern is Catherine, with a slight nod to the children. It would not surprise me at all if she was withholding evidence," Lindsey scowled, scrunching her nose as if smelling something bad. "I believe she hated her husband. They were talking about a divorce, you know."

"I do know, and I sensed her withholding when we talked. She was not at all forthcoming, and, with all due respect, Lindsey, I don't believe you're being completely forthcoming either. If you weren't involved with Kevin, how would you know so much about his wife and the state of their marriage? The best thing you can do for Kevin and for yourself is to tell me the whole truth. I suspect you loved him, affair, or no affair. I see it in your eyes. I'm asking for complete honesty about this, for Kevin. Tell me everything you know."

Lindsey glared at Rosaline. Was the young student angry with her or just sizing her up? Rosaline wasn't sure. She calmly awaited Lindsey's final determination. After a long pause, the barrier fell. Lindsey nodded; more tears fell, and she poured out her heart.

"We were having an affair," she confessed. "I loved him with all my heart. I had nothing to do with his death—he was the love of my life. Please, Judge Maxwell. I beg you, if Tyler Guthrie did not do this, find out who did," she sobbed.

"I'm so sorry to cause you pain. I see that you loved him. You're a brave young woman, Lindsey," Rosaline assured her.

"The whole professor-student dynamic is my only reason for not being truthful. Everyone responsible for these 'rumors' you mentioned are judging Kevin, judging me, wondering if my accomplishments are tied to our relationship. Were we inappropriate? Sure, but we were in love. He never took advantage of me. If anything, he tried to resist *my* advances. He never changed my grades, gave me anything I didn't deserve or earn, or bribed me in any way. Ours was a true affair of the heart.

"There was no huge betrayal of marital vows. Yes, he was technically cheating, but their marriage was over long before I came into the picture. He rejected her because she was a mean, cold, spiteful bitch, not worthy of the love of a man like Kevin.

"I may be too young and naïve to say this, but Kevin and I shared the type of love that people wait a lifetime to find. The circumstances weren't ideal, but I'd be stupid not to pursue happiness with the man I loved. Do you understand? Have you ever experienced that type of love? It takes your breath away. I miss him, terribly. Please, Kevin needs justice!"

Rosaline was relieved to hear the truth. She was heartened by the fact that Lindsey was willing to divulge it to her. Rosaline, obviously, had a vastly different opinion of Kevin Johnstone, who did, indeed, have an inappropriate relationship with a student. She kept her opinion to herself, for obvious reasons, but she was outraged at his behavior. Nonetheless, he was a *murder* victim. Like him or not, nothing he did justified taking his life. The person she felt sorriest for was Lindsey.

Kevin worked his charmer's magic on the young co-ed. He played with her emotions and convinced her that a lie was the truth. Rosaline doubted that Lindsey Parker was the love of Kevin Johnstone's life. She doubted this was a mutual love affair, as opposed to an illicit sexual liaison. The young co-ed, Rosaline opined, was no more than Kevin's most recent, young sidepiece.

"Not easy to hide true love—difficult to lose it, as well. I'm so sorry for your loss, Lindsey," Rosaline consoled. "Because it was secret, you can't publicly mourn him. It must be an excruciating experience. Where do you go for support? To whom do you pour your heart out?"

"No one." Lindsey trembled, tears flowing. "You are the first, Judge Maxwell. Public disclosure would ruin Kevin's legacy. I don't know where these rumors started, but I am scared they will blossom into the full-scale destruction of his reputation and legacy, as well as an outing of our relationship. If you're here, can the local authorities be far behind?"

"Actually . . . yes . . . because they aren't investigating this. They have their man. He's Tyler Guthrie, an innocent man."

"I can't tell my friends. I can only mourn as a student would mourn a teacher. Catherine, who hated him, has loads of support, while I suffer in silence. It's *awful*."

"Now, you have me. Here's my card. I see your pain and you can always call me to talk. I'm here to listen and support you, whenever you need a comforting shoulder," Rosaline assured.

"I'm so glad I met you. You're a lifesaver. Kevin loved me so much, he turned down a job at another school. He didn't want to leave me. He decided to divorce Catherine and we were going to go public. He showed me the papers—we were going to marry after the divorce became final."

Rosaline bit her tongue. If she could like Kevin any less, Lindsey's words might have had that effect. He was a liar and a cheat, either to Catherine or Lindsey, probably, depending upon the moment, to both. The only person Kevin Johnstone sought to please was Kevin Johnstone. Somehow, by an unknown hand, he was terminated for it.

"I'll bet his wife is involved," Lindsey insisted. "I'd start with that crazy, vindictive witch. I'm certain she suspected he was having an affair. Maybe she was upset about the idea of divorce. I have no doubt she's capable of deliberately causing his death. After all, his demise achieves her goals of child custody and financial gain."

Lindsey had a point—Catherine insisted that she and Kevin were working to resolve their differences and trying to avoid breaking up their family. But what if Kevin changed his mind? Perhaps he decided to go through with the divorce. Rosaline doubted he intended to marry Lindsey, but he was probably ready to dump his wife if he could negotiate favorable terms. What if he communicated that desire to Catherine?

"She's definitely a suspect," Rosaline acknowledged. "And after this conversation. I'll continue to investigate her with a new focus. Anyone else I should be looking at?"

"No. Kevin was charming, smart, kind, loving, a fantastic human being. Everyone on campus liked him. I can't believe this has happened." And, with that, Lindsey Parker burst into tears. Rosaline rose and offered her a hug, which Lindsey readily accepted. The young woman was sobbing, trembling, beside herself with grief. She desperately needed support, a constant shoulder to cry on. Rosaline was happy to offer her temporary shelter from her emotional storm. None of this was Lindsey's fault—she was conned into love by an expert con artist. The more Rosaline probed, the more she resented and disliked Kevin Johnstone.

Lindsey calmed, her tears subsided, and the two women separated. Rosaline placed her hands on Lindsey's shoulders and looked into her eyes so that Lindsey grasped the weight of her words.

"Lindsey, I promise you; I will not rest until I unravel this thing. I will do whatever it takes to see justice done. I cannot allow a killer to escape justice."

"Me either," Lindsey assured. "It's Catherine. I know it is. It's obvious to someone familiar with the two of them and their intense disdain for each other. All we need to do is prove it."

Proof. Whoever offed Kevin Johnstone, proof was a huge problem. Not only did the perpetrator cover his or her tracks well, he or she also framed the perfect fall guy. Tyler Guthrie detested Kevin Johnstone, published his frustrations in writing, argued with him on the day of the murder, and, somehow, left his pen at the scene. Rosaline had *two* daunting tasks: First, she needed to prove Tyler did not commit the crime, then, prove who did. An innocent Tyler Guthrie was essential to persuade the authorities to refocus their inquiry.

"Step one is to prove that Tyler did not kill Kevin," Rosaline advised. "Did you recognize or know anyone else at my lecture?"

"Yes," Lindsey sniffled, surprised at the question. "There weren't many, but there were a few familiar faces. Some were classmates and teachers. Why? What makes you think that people who attended had something to do with Kevin's death?"

"I'm not sure, just a hunch, right now." Rosaline admitted. "Perhaps they can help me prove that Tyler is innocent."

With that, Lindsey pulled out a notebook and pen and began to compile a list of lecture attendees.

Chapter Eleven

After Lindsey calmed and assured Rosaline that she was okay, the former judge left and returned to the prison to visit Tyler Guthrie. She arranged a formal 'attorney-client' meeting, this time, but was nervous about the visit. He was in bad shape the last time she visited—she was concerned he might have gone from bad to worse.

She arrived at the prison early and went through the standard visitor protocol for lawyers. Her purse and other possessions were scanned separately. Rosaline walked through a metal detector. She hated the impersonal process, being treated like a criminal, like she was being judged, rather than judging others. She would endure almost any inconvenience to visit and provide some measure of comfort to Tyler.

After a diligent search, she was pronounced 'clean' and permitted to visit the inmate. A guard led her to a small waiting room. Tyler was transferred from a local holding cell to a state prison, but the advantage of having a bar card was that she could still initiate a private visit. She did not have to visit him in a large receiving room with the other inmates and visitors.

When the time came, all visitors were led into the receiving room. White plastic tables and grey, grimy walls were the décor of the day. Rosaline trailed behind the other visitors, but when she got to the entrance, she stopped a guard.

"Attorney Rosaline Maxwell to see inmate Tyler Guthrie." The guard turned and mumbled something into a walkie-talkie. The box squawked back, but Rosaline could not make out the words. The guard told her to have a seat at one of the long white tables. Rosaline separated herself from the others by as much distance as possible and nervously awaited Tyler's arrival. This was not her first prison visit, but this one was different. This was her best friend, Tyler, and she was personally invested.

The inmates were brought in slowly, a few at a time. Their loved ones were supportive and happy to see them, emotions that were not always reciprocated. She glanced over at a few families, wondering about them and their stories. What circumstances brought them to this place? Were these inmates innocent too? She was sure that family members supported their loved ones, believed them to be innocent. She was also sure that most inmates who proclaimed their innocence were lying. Was Tyler lying, too? The question haunted her. Time stood still, as Rosaline waited 'forever' to catch a glimpse of Tyler coming out from the bowels of the prison.

She heard a clang from behind the prison entry door and Tyler Guthrie, in shackles and chains, was walked into the room. He looked hallow and hapless as they dragged him in.

His attending guard looked down at a sheet of paper he was holding onto, looked up, and shouted, "Attorney Rosaline Maxwell?" Rosaline stood and waved her arms. "Here!"

She walked over to the two men. As she approached, she was horrified to discover that the nearer she got to Tyler, the worse he looked. He was gaunt, haunted somehow, looking like he had a terminal illness. He lost a significant amount of weight and his condition had deteriorated more rapidly than she expected. His eyes fluttered, he blinked uncontrollably, and badly needed a shave and shower. When he greeted her, his speech was slurred and slow, foggy, almost as if he suffered a stroke.

The guard led them to the back of the receiving room where Rosaline reached a trio of small, enclosed rooms with electronically controlled doors. As the only attorney-visitor at that moment, Rosaline was offered her choice of rooms. For no particular reason, she chose the one in the middle. A steel metal table sat in the middle of the room, with metal loops soldered to one side. The guard pulled Tyler to that side of the table, unhooked his hand restraints, re-hooked them to the table, and ordered Tyler to sit.

He's not a dog, asshole, Rosaline bristled, silently. She sat down opposite him. The guard stood in the room, off to the side. Rosaline immediately addressed his continued presence.

"The purpose of the room and the door is for attorneys to visit their clients in private. May we please have the room?"

"Sorry," the guard apologized, with what seemed to be genuine remorse. Rosaline wondered how many rookie attorneys fell for this scam, only to face these guards in court, repeating every word the client said in confidence. The guard exited the room, and the attorney and her client had as much privacy as they might expect in this setting. Rosaline studied Tyler.

"It's happening again, isn't it, Tyler? The depression is seeping in, slowly. You are entitled to visit the clinic and to see a shrink. He can prescribe the necessary medication. You don't have to live like this."

"I'm in *prison*, Rosaline. Is anything more depressing than prison? Not much I can do to improve my situation. I'm trying to stay positive, but it becomes more difficult with each passing day. The hardest part is that I'm *innocent*. No one will listen. The cops have made up their minds about me. They seem to find more and more evidence, each day, piling it on. I'm *drowning*, Rosaline. It's a spiral I can't stop myself from falling into. You're my first visitor." He tried to smile.

"I read your book about innocent people going to prison— what happened to those people was awful, spending wasted years in prison for crimes they didn't commit. Still, it's one of those terrible things that happens to others—I never once considered that it might happen to me.

"Their prison exit interviews were remarkable. They were so positive, most were not vindictive, just happy to be released from those horrible places. I don't have that kind of strength. I won't live through years of incarceration and torment. I'm innocent! I won't make it, Roz. You've got to get me out of here."

As Rosaline studied Tyler, the obvious pain he was in, she felt helpless. His words were devastating, a sharp dagger in the pit of her stomach. But he spoke the truth—his mental health would not survive much more. His condition had deteriorated so quickly, Rosaline needed to solve this crime as quickly as possible, before Tyler suffered what could be a permanent breakdown.

"Please Tyler, you mustn't give up," she pleaded. "You're strong, Tyler. The strongest person I know. We are going to solve this thing. I've been working, day and night. I have several leads and suspects. Hang in there for me, please?"

"I'm trying, Rosaline. It's so hard . . ." He drifted away, in obvious pain.

"Viable alternate suspects are the keys to your freedom. Can you think of anything or anyone who might prove your innocence?"

Tyler snapped out of his temporary zone out. "I've been racking my brain. Each new piece of information points to me as the perpetrator. I have no idea what to do."

After periods of initial doubt, Rosaline was fully committed to Tyler's innocence. How do they go about proving it? To prove him innocent, did she have to solve the crime? She pondered strategy.

"We need to make a timeline," she determined. "A timeline would be most helpful. There was quite a crowd at the lecture. How many people used that staircase between the time of the lecture and the time the body was discovered?"

"Hundreds! Thousands! It's hopeless, Rosaline," Tyler commiserated.

"Stop talking like that!" She scolded. "A timeline—we hunt down everyone who saw you and Kevin on campus before and around the time the crime was committed. Perhaps we can identify someone who saw you exit the staircase or leave the area at the same time someone else last saw Kevin alive. Forensics has established the time of death. If we can create a timeline that places you elsewhere at the time of death, we can prove your innocence, without solving the crime.

"If we prove your innocence, you're out of here, whether there's an alternate suspect or not. You won't have to suffer like this much longer. What do you think?"

"That sounds impossible," Tyler challenged. "Remer and the other cops think I'm guilty. They aren't going to invest their time into something like this. They've got their man. At this point, they're only looking for facts to back up their ridiculous assumptions."

"We're not going to rely on the cops," Rosaline resolved. She concluded that proving him innocent, based on his declining mental health, was more important than identifying the killer. And if the cops wouldn't help, she'd do this herself . . .

"I'm going to create my own timeline, determine the whereabouts of everyone on campus, investigate, and prove you innocent of this horrible crime."

"Tracking down all of those people? Making a timeline? How the hell is one *amazing* person going to all that? And you are amazing, Rosaline. But this is too much, even for you, superwoman."

"I'll decide what is or is not too much. You're not the boss of me," she mimicked a child. "It's what needs to be done and what I'm going to do. If I'm willing to invest the time, I need something from you."

"What's that?"

"I need you to invest time into taking care of yourself and developing a more positive outlook. I can't do what is necessary if I'm constantly worrying about your mental health. Can you commit to riding this out, seeing a professional? You must promise me."

"I promise."

Rosaline and Tyler spent the next hour or so going over Tyler's activities and movements on the day of the murder. Where did he go? Who did he see? What events or appointments were on his calendar at or near the time of death? When they completed the exercise, Rosaline continued, head down, writing, vigorously, in a notebook. Tyler studied and smiled at Rosaline. She sensed him staring at her.

"What?"

"Thank you for doing this for me. You truly are a superwoman."

Rosaline flexed her muscles. "Yeah, right, that's me!"

Tyler laughed out loud, a hearty laugh. Rosaline smiled and chuckled in response.

"It's amazing to hear you laugh again, Tyler. Your laugh is contagious," she smiled again.

"There was a time when I thought I would never laugh again. You've given me a little bit of hope, and I appreciate it."

"Just a little bit?"

"I'm cautiously optimistic. How about that? At least I have one person in my corner."

"Hang in there, kid. You can handle anything. You're Tyler Guthrie. Chin up!"

Tyler lifted his chin, straining his neck to lift his head as high as possible. They both laughed a second time. Rosaline came around the table to offer a hug.

"No physical contact!" Came a voice over the intercom. "Visitors and inmates are allowed no physical contact." The door opened, and a guard entered. Rosaline hadn't paid attention to the intercom. *Is it one-way or two?* She shook off the notion. Besides, nothing was incriminating in the conversation.

"Sorry, we forgot," Rosaline apologized.

"Visitor privileges can be suspended for this."

"I got a bit carried away—didn't mean to violate the rules. Again, I'm so sorry." She condescended.

"Is your visit over?" The guard snipped.

Rosaline glanced at Tyler. He did not want her to leave. "Yes," he whispered. "I have some reading to do. And this lady has a lot of work to do."

"Yes, I do. See you soon, Tyler. Remember, try to think positive thoughts!"

"I will. A promise is a promise." He raised his chin again. The two laughed—the guard seemed confused.

"Inside joke," Rosaline explained.

"Whatever," the guard grumbled. He unchained Tyler from the table, reattached his restraints, and called for the inside guards to open the gate. Rosaline Maxwell watched Tyler Guthrie and the guard walk down the prison hallway until they disappeared from view.

Rosaline spent the next several days creating her timeline. Who was on campus at the same time as Tyler and Kevin? Who ran into whom during the day? Investigators wouldn't take her word for the timeline, so she had to buttress it with video cell phone recordings or sworn witness statements. She made lists, tracked down each person, persuaded them to talk, verified statements by matching them up with others, obtained contact information, and consolidated her findings into a cogent presentation. She also included a list of people who refused to cooperate, hoping the cops might follow up. One of those people might be the killer.

This was a painstakingly slow process. Some people refused to talk, others were less than forthcoming, still others were hard or impossible to locate. She poured heart and soul into the presentation until she had what she believed to be a compelling case to present to whomever would listen to reason.

As compelling as her presentation was, she had one more worry. Would anybody at headquarters listen? Judges were trained not to pre-judge the cases brought in their courts. They were required to keep an open mind and make decisions based only on the evidence heard or presented in court. But they were human—it was impossible to have no preconceived notions about a defendant's guilt or innocence. In her years on the bench, Rosaline always did her best to overcome such notions and decide cases based solely on the evidence.

Cops had similar responsibilities. Their job was to identify the *guilty* and put them away. The best cops cringe at the prospect of incarcerating innocent people. So, would Remer and others read or study the material? They seemed content to focus on Tyler. They had their man and were intent on putting him away for life. Could anything she did or said change the direction of the criminal probe? She hung her head. *Probably not.* But she decided to head to the station anyway.

She approached the desk and asked for Detective Remer, surprised that the desk sergeant did not request her name. After a short wait, Remer came strolling out of the 'pit,' spotted Rosaline, and grimaced. He was not exactly thrilled to see her, but he consented to the visit and escorted her to his office. She wondered how he treated ordinary citizens. Did he indulge her because she was an attorney and former judge? If so, she was appreciative of her pedigree.

As they walked to the office, she thought of her book research. Most people had no access to important resources or people available to prove their innocence. They had to rely on overworked public servants with huge unsolved caseloads. If Tyler had no Rosaline, what chance did he have? Her heart went out to anyone going through a similar experience.

"Before you say anything, Rosaline, I must tell you that we have conducted an extensive examination of the evidence, and everything we've found only further confirms Guthrie's guilt." The detective shut the door and offered her a seat. "What can I do for you today? I hope you're ready to admit that your friend did the crime and must do the time.

"He's guilty; I understand it's difficult to hear. I know you two go way back . . ."

"I can *prove* his innocence," Rosaline interrupted. "I've done my due diligence, the way you should have, instead of pre-judging the case and letting conspiracy theories guide your decision-making. Contrary to your conclusions, mine are based exclusively on the evidence."

"Is that so?" Remer crossed his arms over his chest and leaned back in his chair, amused. Rosaline fumed at his arrogance.

"Yes, that is so," Rosaline boasted.

She opened her briefcase, removed and presented her evidence. Her timeline contained piles of evidence, statements, schedules, events, and locations. At the end of it all, Rosaline made a compelling case that Tyler and Kevin were nowhere near each other at the time of Kevin's death. Two witnesses specifically spotted Tyler far away from the staircase, at the same time witnesses saw Kevin approach it.

"I have no clue, yet, who killed Kevin Johnstone, but I can conclusively prove that Tyler Guthrie did not," Rosaline huffed.

"It isn't only the word of one or two witnesses, the evidence is *overwhelming*. If you believe in justice, Detective Remer, about truth, and innocent until *proven* guilty, you cannot ignore this evidence."

Remer blanched, embarrassed. Rosaline's timeline and extensive research were something the cops should have done from the onset. He picked up her thick file and began to leaf through it, silently and deliberately reviewing the evidence. Rosaline remained silent for the better part of an hour as Remer scoured the files.

"I must concede, this is an interesting presentation of the evidence. Of course, I will have to follow up, re-interview all these people, and confirm all these times, events, and appointments. Make sure that everyone was where these various witnesses say they were.

"The brass thinks we've caught the guy—case closed. They're going to say you've written down a bunch of names and numbers to obtain Guthrie's release. I have to confirm and reconfirm everything you've presented," Remer advised.

"And if it checks out?" Rosaline was positive it would check out.

"If it checks out, based on what I just read, Guthrie must be innocent." Remer conceded. "Rosaline, we've had our differences—you aren't happy with the way we went about this— perhaps we got it wrong. But, rest assured, no one in this department wants to pin a crime on an innocent man. I will share this evidence with my captain and call you as soon as possible.

You have my word." Remer promised, his arrogance a distant memory.

"I will hold you to that, Detective," Rosaline pledged.

"I'm sure you will," Remer sighed. "Now skedaddle out of here and let me convince the brass that your client is innocent."

"I'm out of here!" Rosaline leaped up and began to jog out of his office.

"Hey, Rosaline?"

"Yes?" She stopped.

"Glad you set me straight. I work hard to only lock up the bad guys, but, sometimes, bad shit happens. If this checks out, you saved my ass and prevented a tremendous miscarriage of justice." Remer was truly contrite.

"Pleased I was able to assist. I'll leave you to it."

A satisfied Rosaline joyfully skipped out of the station, content to wait for Remer's call to head to the prison and retrieve the newly released Tyler Guthrie.

Chapter Twelve

A week later, on a beautiful sunny day, Tyler Guthrie was released from prison. No one ever hugged Rosaline as tight as Tyler when he ran to her from the open prison gate. It was wonderful to see the golden sunlight hit his face. He was gleaming. He appeared worse than the last time she saw him, but the twinkle in his eye and a huge sigh conclusively demonstrated the relief of being proven innocent. The burden of criminal charges and a potential life sentence were miraculously lifted from his shoulders. Rosaline was confident that time would heal the wounds suffered from this horrible experience. He was going home. It was all that mattered.

They separated after a long embrace. "Oh, Rosaline! Rosaline, Rosaline, *Rosaline*! How can I ever repay you?" Tyler grabbed her and hugged her again, planting a huge kiss on her cheek. "There are no words to express how grateful I am for your hard work and dedicated friendship. 'Superwoman' is an understated description of the super-hero that is Rosaline Maxwell!"

"Jeez, Tyler," she blushed. "Flattery will get you *everywhere*. You're quite welcome, by the way. I did nothing you wouldn't have done for me."

"I would have tried, but I'm not sure I would have succeeded. You are *amazing!*"

"Aw, shucks," she deflected. "I'm just grateful that you are coming home."

Tyler stood in the sunlight, held his arms out, and soaked in the fresh air, enjoying the initial moments of his freedom. The two friends walked arm-in-arm to Rosaline's RV and drove away from the prison, hopefully, forever.

The ride back to campus began in silence. Rosaline glanced over to Tyler a couple of times—he seemed to be enjoying the passing scenery.

"It's wonderful to be free!" Tyler exclaimed. "I thought I was doomed to spend the rest of my life in prison. What a terrible place—how do others do life in a place like that?" Tyler Guthrie began to sob, robust sobs of relief, crying as though he would never stop. Rosaline gave him his moment, his space to let it out and begin the healing process. She pointed to the glove compartment. Tyler opened it and pulled out a package of tissues. He was calming. He wiped his eyes and blew his nose.

"My life is still a nightmare," he sobbed. "How many people on campus still think I'm guilty? I've still got the cheating scandal to deal with and all those rumors. I want to return to being a university president. If I can be set up for murder, I can be set up for a cheating scandal, right? The board should take that into account, right? In the meanwhile, I need some time to unwind, time to myself, let the board's own probe prove my innocence."

"You do need quality time to help recover from this ordeal. Come out and stay at my house for a while. Enjoy the solitude of the lake. Your life was ripped apart. Time heals all wounds—take some time to heal," Rosaline suggested. "Hopefully, the cops will invest their time and resources into finding Kevin's killer and everything will return to normal."

"How's that going? Have you heard anything from Remer? How is the search going? Any progress?" Tyler probed.

"Nothing from Remer, nothing on my end, at least. Molasses," Rosaline reported. "These things take time when the cops don't rush to judgment. Besides, I'm not as motivated now that you've been released. Proving your innocence was far more important than finding the killer, in my book. Maybe we just let the cops do their thing. They're embarrassed and motivated to correct past mistakes. Perhaps we can count on them to do the right thing."

"Finding the killer may not be personal to you, Rosaline, but it is to me. This dangerous person is now roaming around my beloved campus. Hell, the guy may be a serial or repeat offender. Everyone is in danger. I can't give this up. We have to find this guy and Remer's crew hasn't done shit," Tyler urged.

"What are you suggesting, Tyler? You just got released from prison. You lack the skills to personally investigate the crime.

Besides, you need time to heal. You need a break. Let the investigators do their jobs and then reassess. Please?"

"I can't, Rosaline. It's true I despised Kevin. He made my blood boil, but he was my employee, killed on my campus, on my watch. I won't rest until his case is solved. Kevin deserves justice."

Rosaline was touched and a bit surprised by the speech. Whatever their differences, Tyler did not wish Kevin dead. Arrogance, cheating, scandal, whatever, his naughty behavior did not warrant the death penalty. But why the turnaround? Tyler detested Kevin, didn't he?

"Why all this sudden concern about Kevin?" Rosaline asked.

"On campus, he was my responsibility. I wanted him *fired*, not *dead*." Tyler argued. "As I said, it's more than just Kevin. The safety of my students is paramount. There's a killer on my campus and I can't rely on the authorities."

"But maybe the perp just had something against Kevin Johnstone. After all, Kevin was quite a jerk," Rosaline postulated. "The site of the murder might be irrelevant to the crime."

"But what if that isn't the case? What if this is just the start of a series of killings on my campus? What if Kevin isn't the only intended victim? Once scrutiny subsides, this psychopath might strike again. As school president, it is my duty to see that the guy is caught."

Rosaline considered Tyler's words. He continued to be tormented by the professor's death. As she pulled the RV up Tyler's driveway, she sat for a moment to process. He would probably take this on, with or without her. She was concerned he would not be able to handle the strain.

"Well, Tyler," she decided. "I'm in."

"What do you mean, 'in?'"

"I mean you and I will work on this together and find Kevin's killer."

"I'm not trying to guilt trip you, Rosaline."

"But guilt trip me you did. Where would you like to begin?"

Tyler laughed. "With a shower, some food delivery, a very long conversation, and one more thing, Rosaline."

"What's that?"

"Thanks for everything, especially for believing in me."

"What are friends for?"

"If I had a nickel . . ."

They ordered a pizza and waited for the delivery. Tyler was in the shower and Rosaline pulled out her laptop. She could relax, almost at home in his house. Their décor was similar with light blue walls, grey floors, and white furniture. In fact, back in the day, they helped each other design the two homes.

As she sat, reviewing pages of information, her cell phone rang.

"Rosaline Maxwell, how may I help you?"

The voice on the other end of the line sounded like she was fearful. A shaky Lindsey Parker on the other end of the phone uttered, "I'm so glad you picked up. I remembered something. Probably thought about it when we last spoke, but I was too scared to share. After many sleepless nights, I realize I need to tell you."

"What were you afraid of?" Rosaline probed. "I'm harmless. Besides, I'm *retired.* I won't judge you." She tried to lighten the mood.

Lindsey missed the attempt at humor. "No, no! it has nothing to do with you. Kevin is dead. Someone killed him. Given the situation and my suspicions, I could be next. *That's* why I'm terrified. I might be risking my life talking to you."

"Understood, so what did you want to share?"

"I loved Kevin. I miss him terribly and would have done anything to save him. I'd exchange my own life for his if that were possible. I'm willing to do whatever it takes to bring his killer to justice."

Lindsey paused, breathing so heavily that Rosaline heard her breath sounds over the phone. She waited patiently, but anxiously, to hear the big reveal.

"Catherine is hiding something," Lindsey blurted.

Not exactly front-page news, Rosaline thought. *The mistress is suspicious of the wife. Surprise! What else is new?*

"You told me that last time we talked, Lindsey. I already knew how it was between you and Catherine."

"Kevin warned me about her. That's the new part."

"Warned you how? What exactly did he say?"

"He didn't say—he texted. I have the texts," she advised.

Rosaline sat up, now interested in Lindsey's story.

"I'll send them to you. You be the judge," Lindsey offered.

Rosaline was excited, but she didn't want to sound too excited.

"You have my number. Send over the texts and I'll take a look," she suggested.

"Here they come. Call me when you finish."

The texts began to transmit, one by one, text after text. Rosaline was buoyed. Written evidence was far better than testimonial evidence. People can lie, embellish, twist the truth, but once something is in writing . . .

While waiting for Tyler to finish his first solo shower in forever, Rosaline began to read the texts. The more she read, the more disturbed she became.

The first text was sent five months before his death:

I think Catherine is cheating. I have that suspicion. My guess is that she found out about us, and this is her way of exacting revenge. How stupid is this woman? Pathetic, actually. I love you, and only you. Who gives a shit if she fools around?

Similar texts demonstrated that Kevin was suspicious of Catherine. He believed she was having her own affair, feigned a lack of concern that she might leave him. But it obviously pissed him off.

Rosaline was not sure why, but despite his own affair and claimed love for Lindsey, Kevin was livid that his wife was cheating. Perhaps it disgusted him to imagine her with another man. Apparently, this narcissist expected *all* the women in his life to love only him. His failure to reciprocate, apparently, did not occur to him.

His texts began to gather steam:

I'm putting together more evidence about the affair. I tailed her and snapped a few pictures of suspicious behavior. I showed up at her workplace—she was gone. This will affect the property settlement and custody terms. I'll demand custody and the judge will give her shit. She's doing me a tremendous favor behaving like this. You and I will have to stop seeing each other for a while. It's for the best. We can be together when all of this is over, happily ever after, my darling.

Lindsey's responses suggested that she bought everything Kevin was selling. Initially, she tried to convince Kevin to ignore the affair and not worry about the divorce settlement. All that mattered was their love affair. She wanted Kevin to focus on *their* relationship, not the failed one he was leaving behind. Soon, however, she caved. She understood his need to be with his children and to hang on to his precious assets. She missed the big picture. To Kevin Johnstone, this wasn't about the kids or the money. He only wanted to punish Catherine for her naughty behavior. Blinded by love, Lindsey would do anything Kevin wanted and buy any story he was selling.

A month before Kevin's death, he sent Lindsey a text that caused Rosaline's eyes to widen:

*I'm ready to confront Catherine about her affair. First, I'll talk to my lawyer, just to make sure I'm on the right legal track for things to work in my favor. The shit will hit the fan when she's served with the divorce complaint and discovers that I can prove she's having an affair. She'll do anything to keep the kids. **Anything!** I don't want to end up a corpse on some John Walsh true crime documentary. Is Catherine capable of the ultimate crime? Against her own husband? I guess we'll find out . . . Ha!*

Rosaline read and re-read the text. Someone was lying. Neither party was a pillar of honesty. However, Rosaline knew, for a fact, that Kevin was having an affair. Not so for Catherine; her 'affair' may have existed only in Kevin Johnstone's warped mind.

The end of the text suggested, to Rosaline, at least, that Kevin did not believe that any threat from Catherine was consequential. But his death called everything into question. Was Catherine Johnstone, indeed, capable of murder?

A knock at the door startled her, caused her to jump, and drop the laptop, like a scene out of a cheesy horror film. Considering the circumstances, she was afraid to answer the door. Would Michael Myers or Freddy Krueger be on the other side? She walked to the door, peered into the peephole, and saw a young, pimple-faced kid holding a pizza box. Using her brilliant sleuthing skills, she determined that this was, indeed, the pizza delivery guy. She opened the door, greeted the young man, took the pizza, paid for it, and gave the kid a large tip for not being a stone cold killer.

She laid the pizza on the kitchen counter, found some plates, napkins, and plasticware, and brought all of it back into the living room. Tyler emerged from the bedroom, wearing gym shorts and a tee shirt. The two of them settled down for dinner and a discussion about Catherine Johnstone.

Chapter Thirteen

As they gorged on pizza and guzzled stale beer that Tyler found in the fridge, Rosaline filled Tyler in on what they now called *the Lindsey texts.*

"The evidence points more and more to Catherine," Tyler opined, stuffed with non-prison pizza and buzzed from three bottles of beer. After months in prison, stale beer tasted like fine wine. "You have to wonder why investigators didn't target her in the first place. Don't they *always* focus on the spouse? Why were they so eager to pin this on me?" He wailed.

"She inspires sympathy, at least she did with me," Rosaline noted. "Investigators have their biases. Perps, particularly murderers, are usually men, not women. Besides, you were easy prey with your pen at the scene and those angry rants." She paused and looked Tyler in the eye. "Do *you* think Catherine killed her husband?"

"Difficult to say," Tyler decided, after considering the question. "I've only met her a few times. She was always pleasant and respectful to me. Doesn't seem like someone capable of doing the deed, but, then again, neither am I, and people had no problem believing that of me. Mostly though, I had sympathy for the lady."

"Why?"

"She was married to Kevin Johnstone."

"You aren't supposed to badmouth the dead."

"I can't help it—he was a terrible person. Must have been an awful husband. Besides, texts don't lie," he quipped.

"Even the best people have limits. Kevin certainly tested Catherine's. Besides, maybe it was all an act. Judges are supposed to be able to determine whether people are lying, but it is extremely difficult, sometimes. There are supremely skillful liars. It was easier to spot lies and liars when I was on the bench."

"How so?" Tyler asked.

"Because the opposite side would present a boatload of evidence trying to convince me or a jury that some person was lying. The *evidence* helped to determine the liar, not the demeanor or tell of the person doing the lying. Anyone who tells you he is an expert at spotting a liar is . . . well . . . a liar! I'm certainly no expert at spotting a tell.

"If solving this crime is important to you, I think we would be wise to investigate Catherine Johnstone and Lindsey Parker. They are the most likely suspects with that Tyler guy out of the way," she cracked.

"Not just brilliant, funny too. You are my idol," Tyler gushed.

"Yeah, yeah. Are you sure you don't want to let the investigators handle this?"

"At the same time? Sure, send them the texts and let them do what they do. But this is our best lead, so far, and I want to follow it up. Okay?"

"Okay, Tyler. What do you have in mind?"

Rosaline and Tyler spent the rest of the day plotting strategy and waiting for dark.

When evening fell, the two amateur sleuths climbed into Tyler's car. Tyler was rusty, but he drove to Catherine's house without incident. They chatted about mundane things, seeking distraction from the mission they were embarking upon.

They became silent as they approached the house, parking far enough away to be inconspicuous, but near enough to monitor comings and goings.

"Have you or the cops done anything more about the cheating scandal? Remer was convinced Kevin was blackmailing me about it. Does he now understand it was *Kevin* who was manipulating grades, blackmailing students and other professors, filing false reports of harassment and cheating?" Tyler rambled.

"The Harbor Springs Police have done a deep dive into the academic files of students involved, Professor Johnstone, and others, and conclusively decided that any so-called cheating scandal was either perpetrated or manufactured by Johnstone. Grade-changing for sexual favors? Johnstone. Accusations of cheating against you and other professors or students? Manufactured by Johnstone. You are completely in the clear on both the murder and the cheating scandal."

"That's great news. Complete exoneration—such a relief. Thanks, Rosaline. I hope to repay you someday."

"You're welcome. I'm pleased it all worked out. There were times, dealing with Remer and his team, that I wasn't sure he'd come to his senses. So, we have time on our hands—it's just you and me. Are you enjoying your first day of freedom? Anything you want to talk about?"

Tyler launched into a tirade about prison life and how horrific it is to be locked up in that awful place when you're completely innocent. This was one more reminder of why Rosaline's work and book were so important. Conditions were deplorable, so much so, that Tyler refused to talk about them. He knew he was one of the lucky ones. Rosaline wrote about people who were wrongly incarcerated for *years*.

"And that's why we have to finish this investigation the right way. Although Remer and company finally came around, the local cops have demonstrated lots of stubbornness, a bit of laziness, and an alarming lack of due diligence. They are living up to the old stereotypes about inept, ill-prepared small-town police departments. We must be certain that the right person is captured and punished."

"Spoken like a true diplomat, lawyer, and judge," Tyler quipped.

They were so engrossed in conversation, they almost missed the first sign of movement. A car pulled up and parked parallel to the house, on the opposite side of the street. They leaned forward and watched as the driver exited the vehicle.

"I recognize that kid!" Tyler exclaimed. "He's one of my favorite students. David Barkley. We've worked charity projects together. Always the first to volunteer, friendly, solid grades, smart boy, and very popular. He can't be involved in this, can he? Oh, my God, Roz!"

The pair watched as David meandered up to Catherine's front door. He surveyed the area, suspiciously. He glanced left, right, and looked their way. Rosaline blanched and averted eye contact. She worried that he spotted them.

But all David saw was a dark, parked car. Satisfied that no one was watching him, he knocked on Catherine's door. She opened it and quickly pulled him into the house. Rosaline speculated that Catherine may have been concerned about busybody neighbors, hoping that no one saw the young man. Tyler had a different, far more innocent take on his visit.

"Perhaps he showed up to offer condolences," Tyler suggested. "Is he a friend of the family, a distant relative, or something? His visit is not necessarily nefarious."

"Kevin's death happened quite a while ago, Tyler. I doubt that this is a condolence call."

Obviously, Tyler liked David Barkley. He didn't want the kid to be involved. Because he didn't, neither did Rosaline, and she would not jump to conclusions. Yet, there he was, with Kevin Johnstone's widow. Perhaps his charity work and his brown-nosing with Tyler was a mask to his more devious, criminal side.

"Keep watching. He's on our suspect list. No more, no less. Besides, he's probably somewhere in my evidence folder and the timeline might rule him out," Rosaline offered. "For now, no one is ruled out unless there is proof of innocence."

The car returned to quiet for a while. Tyler broke the somewhat awkward silence.

"Did you believe that about me? I mean, before the timeline, before the evidence of innocence, did you think I might be guilty?"

Rosaline froze. Tyler was still healing—she didn't want to make things worse. She also didn't want to lie. Tyler deserved the truth, positive or negative, however painful.

"Yes, Tyler, I confess I did," she admitted. "As the evidence mounted, with the pen in plain sight at the crime scene, I considered the possibility. But not necessarily because I thought you were guilty. I was concerned with helping you if you were *found* guilty. You understand what I mean? There's a huge difference.

"Whatever the truth was, I committed to helping you through this nightmare. Second guess you? Maybe, but in my heart, I never believed you were capable of murder."

Tyler nodded in appreciation. The car fell silent again as they waited for David to leave Catherine's home. The shades were drawn increasing speculation and frustration.

"I understand what you're saying, Roz," Tyler ended the silence. "Hell, the cops even made *me* think I might be guilty, like I blacked out or something. Still, you fought for me when everyone else thought I was guilty. And you *proved* me innocent. That's far better than 'not guilty,' right? No one, not even my enemies, can ignore absolute proof of innocence. I owe you."

"You paid for the pizza and provided that delicious beer. We're even. Give it a rest, will you, please?"

"Okay, but I still say you're a superhero."

"Have it your way. But it was my duty. You're innocent and you didn't deserve that. Catherine, though . . ."

They continued to chat about the case and the challenges the school faced moving forward. Another hour passed. Tyler began to wonder what was going on inside the home. He was incredibly bored, extremely antsy, engaging in rank speculation about a possible sexual liaison between David and Catherine. At first, Rosaline tried to talk him down, but the longer David remained in the house, the more Rosaline began to concur with Tyler's suspicions.

"What do *you* suppose they're doing in there?" Tyler wondered.

"She's a recent widow. Kevin's death is still somewhat fresh. I find it hard to believe she's having sex with a student." Rosaline shook her head.

"Maybe that student is why Kevin is dead. Ever think of that? Maybe they're in this together," Tyler speculated.

"You're suggesting that Catherine is a cougar and David is the person Kevin suspected?"

"Isn't it possible? Probable even? In the 21st Century, anything goes."

"We can certainly investigate their relationship. Follow David around campus, talk to Remer about him. Or, maybe, hire a private investigator."

"I'll spring for the investigator," Tyler offered. "Remer and his crew are worthless."

"There is *something* going on between them, that's for sure. We need to find out what that something is, one way or the other. I'm exhausted. I don't think it's worth waiting for David anymore tonight. If your suspicions are true, he may be there until morning. Let's hit the road."

They began the ride back to Tyler's house. Roz glanced over to him—he was sorting things out in his mind. He was muttering to himself when he turned to her.

"I'm the school president. David likes and respects me. What if I call him into the office, have a talk with him? Maybe he'll come clean about their relationship. This is a good kid with a kind heart. If we can figure out the right approach, I think he'll talk," Tyler suggested.

"It's worth a try, I guess, unless he and the cougar are guilty," Rosaline pointed out the obvious.

"Yeah, there's that. That's the downside."

"Even good people can sometimes do the wrong things. I don't want you playing Lone Ranger with David Barkley. If you insist on talking to him, I want to be there. Maybe, we should hire that investigator, and invite him or her to the party. Anyone come to mind?"

"No. It's not my world."

"It *is* my world, and I just thought of someone. He retired about six months ago. Still in the area. Want me to reach out? The guy owes me a favor or two. Maybe he'll do this on the cheap."

"What the hell? Reach out. The worst he can do is say no."

"Will do."

They soon arrived back at Tyler's house. Tyler went into the house. Rosaline walked to the RV and drove home, completely exhausted, worried that she might fall asleep at the wheel.

She arrived home safely, parked the RV, and headed for the front door. She began her climb up the stairs, abruptly stopping in her tracks. There was another handwritten note. Different handwriting this time, loopy, messy, almost as if it was written by a child. Most likely, it was written that way to hide the identity of the author. The words were chilling.

I know you're following me, watching me. But I'm watching you too. Drop this case or the next body found in the stairwell might be yours.

Chapter Fourteen

Rosaline found it impossible to sleep. The words of the note taunted her, disrupted her sense of safety in her own home. When she was a judge, she received death threats from time to time, which goes with the territory, particularly when dealing with criminals and controversial cases. But, once she left the courtroom, home was her safe zone.

A predator invaded her *home*, threatened her with death. Whoever this was, he or she knew where she lived. This was not something she could ignore. If this *was* the person who ended Kevin Johnstone's life, that person would not hesitate to kill again if he or she felt threatened.

She considered her options. Go to Remer? He would arrange protection, whatever protection a small-town department could provide. But Remer would discover she was still on the case. He might resent her continued involvement. He might order her to stay off the case. She quickly ruled out a visit to the cops.

Should she convince Tyler to drop the whole thing? Her goal was to exonerate Tyler and that goal had been accomplished. Why not leave the rest to Remer and his cronies on the force? The problem was that Tyler wouldn't let it go. He'd continue on his own. Besides, was she going to let a bully threaten her off the case?

Still, she had to earnestly consider the threat. If this was Kevin's killer, he or she was willing to kill to conceal hidden secrets. And if someone else was in the crosshairs, Rosaline did not want to be responsible for another person's death.

Apparently, she dozed off, because her next conscious thought came as the sun began to peek over the horizon where the lake met the sky. It was a stunning view, a cascade of colors, blue, green, yellow, red, and orange. She paused, wondering how such beauty could coexist with chaos and pure evil.

She boiled water, made herself a cup of tea, walked out onto the porch, and watched the sunrise dance along the lake. She decided that she had to solve this case. She would call Charlie Granger, her PI friend. When she told him the circumstances, he would be eager to help. The best way out of danger is to confront it, head on, and that's what Rosaline Maxwell intended to do. No one was going to threaten her off the case.

Rosaline needed to expose the killer before he or she had any chance to realize she was still investigating. She finished her tea and headed for the shower, lingering in the hot spray longer than usual, luxuriating, thinking, considering her mode of attack. As the water began to chill, she stepped out of the shower, blow dried her hair, dressed, and headed out the door. She felt better as she headed for Tyler's house.

As soon as she saw Tyler, she showed him the note. His house smelled like bacon and coffee, and she realized how hungry she was. Neither of them had eaten since they shared a pizza the afternoon before. The two friends enjoyed breakfast, then took their coffee out to Tyler's back porch. Once again, the Johnstone situation reared its ugly head.

"This is scary, Rosaline. I'm out of prison and no longer a suspect. You accomplished what you set out to do. Finding the killer is not worth your life. I want you to stop what you're doing. I'll handle things from here."

"And you will become the target of this same deranged individual. There is no way I'm going to let you do that. Neither of us will rest until this person is behind bars. Let's discuss our next steps, shall we?"

"Next steps?"

"Yes. We investigate, but we do so wisely, safely, and in a way that no one realizes he or she is being investigated."

"I like the sound of that. What do you have in mind?"

"I presume we agree that we can't rely on local law enforcement?"

"One hundred percent. They're lazy, sloppy, and every other negative adjective I can think of."

"I guess that rules out going to the police," she chuckled. "There's this guy I know. I told you about him. Used to be a cop, then a private investigator, now retired, Charlie owes me a favor.

When I tell him what's going on, the shoddy support we got from the Harbor Springs locals, I'm sure he'll jump in with both feet."

"If you believe in this guy, that's good enough for me."

"We continue to investigate. Run everything through Charlie. The killer knows us but not Charlie. We plan, Charlie implements. What do you think?"

"I like it."

"I haven't been able to confirm this, but I have to believe someone is following me. How else would the killer know I was still investigating the case? I want to head to campus or stay here and camp out. I'm good, either way. In any event, I will call Charlie, and fill him in on the status of the investigation. If I head for his office and this guy is following me, he will know we involved Charlie and that might put *Charlie* in danger, too."

Tyler was hesitant but eventually agreed. There was no stopping Roz when she set her mind to something. Because of campus security, they decided it would be safer to head to the university rather than run things from Tyler's house. They hopped into Tyler's car and headed toward campus. They continued to plot as they drove. Rosaline would use a spare office close to Tyler's, to call Charlie. Tyler would arrange an interview with David Barkley.

"I don't like you doing this on your own, Tyler. What if David's the guy? What if he penned the note?"

"There is no way David Barkley killed a college professor, Roz, even one as vile as Kevin Johnstone. No way."

"But, if he is the guy, you're putting yourself in grave danger. That's the exact opposite of what we discussed. Why should I take a step back if you won't?"

"Because he'll have no idea that I'm investigating him. Leave it to me. I'm going to leave my cell on speaker, and you can listen in on the entire conversation. If you think I'm missing something, call my cell. I'll pretend it's a business call."

"I can think of a thousand ways this goes wrong, Tyler. Why not hire Charlie and have him confront the kid?"

"Because he's a kid! And my gut says he's not involved. He's my student and we do this my way, or not at all. As to the rest, I'll defer to you and Charlie. I promise. Deal?" This was no request, Tyler was laying down the law.

"Deal. So much for the partner approach," Rosaline protested.

"Just on this one kid, Roz."

"Alright, Tyler. I will defer, this one time."

They arrived on campus. As Tyler walked toward the administration offices, he was greeted warmly by many of his students and faculty. After being avoided like a case of COVID, President Guthrie was in vogue again. Tyler was far too happy to be angry.

After setting Rosaline up in the spare office, Tyler checked out David's schedule. He determined which building David's class was in, glanced at his watch, and ran out the door. Class was over in ten minutes, and the building was five minutes away. Tyler had to stop for numerous well-wishers, which caused him to reach the building as class was being dismissed. David saw him as he exited the lecture room.

"Mr. Guthrie! Glad to see you back on campus. I assumed you were going to take some time off."

"David Barkley! Pleased to be seen. Actually, I *am* taking time off. Just here to say hello to a couple of people. Happily, you're now one of them. So . . . hello!"

"Ha! Glad to see your sense of humor remains intact. What they did to you would crush anyone's spirits, but not yours. That's one of the things I love most about this school. Your spirit lives on this campus."

"Wow, David! High praise coming from one of my students. You are too kind."

"Have you been completely exonerated?"

"Yes. They have cleared me. I'll have to work to restore my reputation. I'm sure there are plenty of people who still think I did it. We must find the actual killer."

"We?" David seemed suspicious.

"I'm sorry, a figure of speech. I mean the cops. I was their number one guy, and I didn't do it. They'll have to concentrate on someone else, the widow, perhaps?" They walked away to a quiet garden with a couple of benches. Both men sat down.

"I never believed what everyone was saying. I told everyone I came in contact with. Mr. Guthrie, a killer? No way!"

"Not everyone shared your opinion. This wasn't easy."

"I hope they catch the guy soon. Everyone is on edge."

"When I return to my duties, perhaps the guy will have already been caught or I can take some steps to increase security or otherwise alleviate anxiety on campus."

"Either or both would be nice."

"There is nothing more important than the safety of my students. A nurturing, welcoming and safe environment in which to learn is my number one priority.

"In fact, while the locals are still trying to figure things out, I've been doing a little sleuthing myself," Tyler floated, violating his agreement with Rosaline.

David seemed confused. "Shouldn't you leave that to the pros? With all due respect, sir, you can't investigate a *murder* case."

"Maybe not, maybe so, but the safety of my students is my foremost consideration."

"Glad to hear it. If there's anything I can do to help, please give me a call."

"As a matter of fact, there *is* something you can do. I'd like to talk to you about the case if you don't mind."

As Tyler uttered the words, Rosaline came up to the garden, huffing and puffing as if she ran all the way from the office.

"Tyler! I came by the office. They said you were 'roaming' the campus, whatever that means. Glad I caught you."

"Actually, I was just heading back to the office. David, have you met my friend, Rosaline Maxwell?"

"I have," David acknowledged, turning to her. "Your book is fantastic. I purchased a signed copy. The idea of innocent people spending even a minute in prison is abhorrent. I'm so sorry, Mr. Guthrie, that you had to experience this first-hand."

"I remember meeting you," Rosaline shared, "and your kind words about my book. I admire your passion for the material. I remember our conversation. It's satisfying to discuss the book and the program with someone who shares my interests and beliefs."

"It's a fascinating study of horrible injustices," David advanced. He addressed Tyler. "I was so worried about you, Mr. Guthrie. I thought you might end up a statistic in one of Judge Maxwell's books. Worse, I worried someone might harm you. I'm so glad you came out unscathed."

"Thanks for the kind words, David. Now, about that talk. Will you come back to the office with me?" Tyler glanced at Rosaline who shot him a look. She was livid that he might be putting them in danger.

David attempted to hide his emotions, but he was discomforted. He tried to deflect it with words. "I've got an hour before my next class, Mr. G. Of course, I'll come to the office. Lead the way."

They walked through campus. Tyler again was forced to endure the fond welcomes of well-wishing students and professors. He wondered where all these people were while he was locked up. The only person to visit him in prison was Rosaline Maxwell. After a brisk walk with numerous stops, they were safely inside Tyler's office.

Rosaline sat beside David, facing Tyler, who sat at his desk. The setting was akin to a lawyer whose client was being interrogated. She studied David. Last night, they were parked too far away to see his features. She was surprised how young he looked, with wide, green eyes, perfectly combed blonde hair, and tall, wiry build. *He's a baby!*

David shifted uncomfortably in the chair. Rosaline tried to imagine this kid bumping off another man. She also tried to imagine him penning and delivering a letter that threatened her life—It just didn't fit.

"Roz and I have been privately investigating the death of Professor Johnstone." Tyler began. "After what Harbor Springs tried to do to me, and although I've been exonerated, I'm still motivated to find Kevin's killer. My students and faculty deserve no less. I must ensure their safety. So, I'd like to start by asking you about Professor Johnstone. Did you know him?"

"I've never taken any of his classes. I might have seen him on campus here or there, but that's it. We never met."

"That's strange, your schedule contradicts your words. You had Professor Johnstone last semester. You dropped the class six weeks in. His own records indicate you were doing well in the class. Why would you drop it after working so hard and why would you lie about taking his class?"

Rosaline was impressed and fearful at the same time. So far, this was an excellent interrogation and Tyler would have made a fine cop or investigator. Rosaline was conflicted though, because he may have been confronting a dangerous killer.

"I'm sorry I lied. I wanted to forget the whole experience like it never happened."

Tyler understood how he felt. He felt the same way about Kevin *and* prison. "Yes, I understand, David. But that doesn't excuse a student from lying to the school president."

"I'm terribly sorry, Mr. G. Not too fond of Professor Johnstone. We just didn't . . . what's the word? Mesh. We didn't mesh. While I did well, I hated the class and decided not to continue. I dropped it. I can guess what you're thinking since you're investigating his death, but no, absolutely not, I did not dislike him enough to kill him."

"I understand this is an uncomfortable subject, but I need you to be completely honest with me. Deal?"

"Deal."

"Can you share specifics on what caused friction between you and Professor Johnstone?"

David scratched the back of his neck and shifted in his seat. "He was inappropriate with certain students. Conducted himself in a bad manner. His behavior was repulsive. He was a married man. There were rumors of an extramarital affair with a student. That made me extremely uncomfortable. I felt bad for his family and refused to interact with a lawyer and law professor of such dubious character. That's why I dropped out. He was morally bankrupt and a bad influence."

Tyler nodded as if to understand and appreciate the kid's decision. "That's quite a stance to take, David. Aside from the credits lost, you lost a ton of money. Why not stick with it, finish the class, and never see the guy again?"

"I thought about it, but, in the end, I decided not to."

"Why not? Did his wife have anything to do with your decision?"

"His wife, sir?"

"Yes, you know her, don't you?"

"No."

"But you just said you felt bad for the family."

"I was speaking metaphorically. I put myself in their shoes and felt bad for them. My father cheated on my mother. It's uniquely personal and disturbing to me. Understand where I'm coming from?"

"I do, David, but here's the thing. As part of our fact-finding mission, we were watching Catherine Johnstone's house last night. Me and Rosaline. Roz, do you want to tell David who paid her a visit?"

Tyler appeared angry and disappointed. He had lobbied for David, believed him to be a fine, upstanding young man. She felt bad for her friend but glad his eyes were being opened to the truth.

David's cheeks turned red. His eyes widened. He refused to meet Tyler's gaze. An expression of panic and anger crossed over his face.

"Are you stalking me or something?" he demanded, his demeanor becoming dark and defensive.

Tyler remained calm. "No, David, as I explained earlier. Roz and I maintained surveillance on the Johnstone home. We are investigating her potential involvement in the murder. After all, she's the spouse, there were rumors he was cheating, rumors *she* was cheating, which made her a logical suspect.

"Anyway, we're sitting in our car, parked down the street, and, surprise! *You* show up. You weren't even on our radar, but there you were, scanning your surroundings, making sure you weren't spotted."

David's demeanor remained dark and defensive. Rosaline was convinced he was through cooperating. Would he answer more questions? It seemed unlikely.

"Catherine is my mom's friend," David claimed. "That's why I was at her house that evening—I went over to check on her. She's going through a lot right now, her husband's death, young children to raise, all by herself. She's not a weak woman, but that's a lot for anyone to shoulder by herself. I thought I might help, went over there as a friend to offer my support. Did she need something done around the house? Run an errand or two? That sort of thing.

"It was Mom's idea. She wanted to go herself, but the tragedy spooked her. Thought she'd do more harm than good. So, she sent me, and I went to offer our condolences and assistance."

Rosaline was impressed by the spontaneous explanation for his visit. He was quite believable, but his actions belied his words. He stayed too long at Catherine's home. There was more to his visit than a simple offer of help to a friend in need. Tyler was even more suspicious.

"Condolences and assistance, huh? Are you sure that's all it was?" Tyler snipped.

"Quite sure," David reaffirmed, folding his arms across his chest.

"So, if I called your mom, right now, she would confirm this little story of yours?"

David's smug expression of certainty disappeared. He refused to meet Tyler's glare. When he did, frustration and defiance lined his face.

"What is your deal? Who the hell do you think you are?" David demanded. "I don't answer to you and I don't have to respond to your absurd allegations. What right do you have to interrogate me, treat me like a common criminal? I don't have to tell you a damn thing and I certainly don't have to answer your ridiculous questions."

David was hiding something. Tyler was sure of it. Tyler went into the interrogation believing in David, certain of his innocence. His disappointment was obvious—David was anything but innocent.

"You're quite right, David," Tyler agreed, leaning back in his chair, clasping his hands behind his head. "We're not detectives. You don't have to talk to us or answer questions. In fact, you may leave whenever you wish."

David stood, relieved, ready to part company with his amateur interrogators. He turned to leave.

"The thing is though, talking to us might help you," Tyler advised, causing David to turn back around.

"How in hell will talking with you two help me? Given the tone of this conversation, I believe you suspect me of killing Professor Johnstone. Am I reading the tea leaves correctly?"

"We are not accusing you of murder, nothing of the sort. We're accusing you of lying about your relationship with Catherine Johnstone. You're *involved* with her, somehow. As such, you know more about her than most other people. Do I think you bumped off Kevin? No. But you aren't telling us everything. I'm sure of that, too. And we believe you can help us solve this case.

"The cops, Detective Remer and his crew? You saw how they focused on and treated me. They charged and imprisoned me on flimsy evidence with almost no follow-up. They refused to even consider anyone else. I was their target and they wouldn't let up until Rosaline proved me innocent. They should have made the effort Roz made and proved what she proved, but they preferred to keep me in prison for something I didn't do. Roz saved me—*she* did the detective work to clear my name. If not for her, I'd still be in prison."

"I'm happy for you, Mr. Guthrie, really, I am. But what does all this have to do with me? I repeat. I did not kill Professor Johnstone."

"Let's assume you had an affair with Catherine Johnstone," Tyler speculated. David opened his mouth to protest, but Tyler put a finger to his lips, silencing him. "I'm not saying there was an affair, just speculating about the evidence.

"I'm no longer a suspect—I've been cleared. Investigators are going to be searching for new suspects, digging into the evidence, Kevin's and Catherine's relationships. If, in fact, you *were* having an affair with Catherine, you will become the number one suspect. You'll become the cornerstone of their search for the truth and they might do to you what they did to me. And, if they do, you will need a friend, two friends, perhaps. Do you want Roz and I to work on clearing you or do you want to take your chances with the Harbor Springs Police Department, all on your own, probably from a jail cell, hoping that they will somehow luck into the truth of your innocence? Can you rely on them after seeing the way they treated me?"

David remained mute, appearing to consider Tyler's words. Tyler continued.

"Roz and I are committed to finding the truth. If you had nothing to do with Kevin's death, but agree that you might be a suspect, we are your best bet. But you have to level with us."

Rosaline listened to the conversation, impressed with Tyler's tenacious argument, hoping that his words reached and persuaded David. The young student paced the room, rubbed his forehead, turned, and walked over to Tyler's desk. He sat down and looked Tyler straight in the eyes.

"Okay, you two, I believe you. You've made your case and I have nowhere else to turn. I'll tell you everything." David shut his eyes and sighed. He opened his eyes, appeared to calm, and began to spill his guts.

Chapter Fifteen

"I admit it," he confessed. "I was having an affair with Catherine Johnstone. It's the truth. You must protect me—I don't want to go to jail or be charged with a crime I didn't commit."

"We appreciate your honesty, David. And we've got your back. There's no judgment here. Kevin cheated on Catherine. It is not surprising that Catherine would cheat on Kevin. It's not like you broke up this couple. It is likely that their marriage was over long before you came into the picture. But we have some questions, probably the same ones the cops will have, once they discover the affair. Do you understand?"

"I do. Ask your questions. I'll do my best to answer them."

"Roz?" Tyler invited Rosaline to continue the interrogation. "Let's start at the beginning, David," Rosaline suggested. "How did you meet Catherine?"

"Actually, I sought her out, not as a stalker or anything like that, but because her husband was cheating on her and it pissed me off. My father did the same thing to my mother. It's something I can't tolerate. Even when a friend of mine bragged about cheating on his girlfriend, I ended the friendship. Breaking someone's heart, is a terribly cruel thing to do, don't you think?

"One day, Catherine shows up on campus to visit Kevin. I already know he's cheating on her. I'm approaching his office for opinion about a project I was working on. I see her walk in and I wait outside. Perhaps I was prying, but I listen in on their conversation. He lays on the Kevin Johnstone charm and she eats it up. She doesn't deserve to be betrayed like this—I resolve, then and there, that Professor Johnstone is a terrible person who needs to be punished."

"Punished how?" Rosaline countered.

"I'm not sure, *punished.* Back then, I thought long and hard, desperate to protect her from the hurt and shame she was about to experience. And I didn't want her to stay loyal to some asshole who was cheating on her. A couple days later, I reached out to her on social media and asked her to meet with me to discuss something about her husband."

"She responded to that?" Tyler was astonished.

"She did," David nodded. "Surprised me, too. I believe she was already suspicious of his behavior, seeking evidence of cheating or something. She figured I might have additional information. Whatever the reason, she agreed to the meeting. We met at a coffee shop on campus. I bought her a coffee and cookie and broke the news." David paused, hung his head, with an empathetic, pained expression on his face. His relationship with Catherine Johnstone wasn't some short-term hookup—he believed he *loved* this woman.

"The expression on her face when her suspicions were confirmed . . ." David shook his head in disgust. "It was heartbreaking. She was horrified, in terrible pain, and I was unable to comfort her. It was an awful experience.

"I was patient, though. I listened as she vented about their relationship or lack of one. I told her of my feelings of betrayal when my father, my former hero, cheated on my mother. Gradually, she opened up, confided in me, shared her pain. I was pleased to be there for her, be a confidant, someone to unburden herself to. When she finished her spiel, we went our separate ways, and I assumed that was that."

"How did the affair begin?" Rosaline inquired.

"After the coffee shop meeting, I couldn't get her out of my mind. Yes, she was several years older than me, but she was beautiful and vulnerable. I found myself attracted to her. I reached out by phone. She was terribly depressed. I offered to take her to dinner, perhaps take her mind off things. She hesitated at first, but eventually agreed, as long as we went somewhere off campus.

Our dinner was fabulous. We connected like we were old friends. After that night, we met on a regular basis and I developed a crush on her. Eventually, she reciprocated, and the affair began.

"Perhaps it began as revenge sex. I worried about that. I didn't want to be some sort of consolation prize or rebound trophy. I was falling in love with her. But I sensed that she was falling for me. We plan to marry when all this blows over. It's too soon for her children, but this is far more than some fling."

Rosaline was disgusted. Both Kevin and Catherine were using vulnerable students as pawns in some sick game of heartbreak and false promises. She didn't believe Catherine intended to marry David any more than she believed Kevin intended to marry Lindsey. Both of these children were victims.

"The two of you fell in love. I understand that. You were both in a place where each of you filled a need for the other. You must have been shocked and angry when Catherine decided to work on reconciling with her husband," Rosaline surmised.

David's eyes steeled. His fists clenched in obvious anger. He willed himself to calm. Rosaline wondered whether he was angry enough to commit the ultimate crime.

"That would not have happened," David blurted, trying, in vain, to seem indifferent. "Kevin Johnstone was manipulative, charming even. He and Catherine had children to consider. Perhaps, in a moment of weakness, she consented to give reconciliation a try, but she had no faith he'd ever change his cheating ways. However, she also had to make a showing for the children and for any potential divorce judge. She was desperate to retain custody of her children. There was a substantial income disparity, and Catherine needed alimony and child support to survive. She needed to be the victim of misconduct.

"I was fine with it. After all, she had to protect herself and her kids. They were to be my stepchildren and I wanted the best for them. I'd be patient. At the end of the day, she did not love him."

Rosaline considered his words. While he was naïve about the adult relationship, he caused Rosaline to shift her focus. If Catherine hated Kevin and feared losing her kids and her support, these were compelling motives. But David had an equally potent motive. With Kevin out of the way, Catherine would be his. Perhaps they plotted and implemented the crime together. Was there anything he wouldn't do for the woman he loved?

"She wouldn't hurt him, Judge Maxwell. While she no longer loved him, he was her children's father. They were discussing a shared custody arrangement. She wanted him to be a part of her children's lives."

Rosaline's head was spinning. The boy would make a fantastic lawyer someday. His argument was compelling, sensical, truthful sounding. Tyler was skeptical and considered both of them prime suspects, but he decided not to be accusatory. He wanted David to continue to converse openly and honestly about the relationship.

"The story makes perfect sense, David. We have a long way to go with this thing. I'm sure you understand, considering the circumstances, that you would both be suspects if Remer and his detective buddies found out about the affair. We must clear you like Rosaline cleared me. Can you prove your whereabouts at the time of the murder? Can Catherine?" Tyler demanded.

David considered the question and shrugged, helplessly. "Probably not," he admitted. "I attended Judge Maxwell's lecture. Someone may have seen me on campus at some point. Everyone uses that staircase, as I certainly did, but I did not see the professor and it was well before the cops say he died. Here's the truth:

There's a reason no one can place me on that stairwell at the time of the murder. I didn't kill him, nor did I have anything to do with his death."

"We need to confirm that, David. Meanwhile, can you think of anyone you may have crossed paths with that day?" Tyler queried.

David gave them the names of people he interacted with at the lecture and immediately following the event. He mentally traced the aftermath and provided a few more names but was unable to confirm his whereabouts at the time of the murder. The amateur sleuths had some names and a starting point. They were grateful for his cooperation and content with his story.

"Glad to get this stuff off my chest and out in the open," David sought to wrap up their conversation. "I did not do this. Neither did Catherine. I was no fan of Professor Johnstone—a lot of people, faculty, administration, and students, felt the same, you included, Mr. Guthrie. That doesn't make us criminals. There's a huge difference between disliking or even hating someone and being capable of *this*. I didn't kill him—I knew you didn't either."

"I believe you, kid," Tyler assured him. "We'll solve this thing, one way or another. Can't have you living in fear of going to prison. In the meantime, can you think of anyone else who might have had a motive to off Kevin?"

"How about his lover?" David suggested. "Was she aware that the professor was reconciling with his wife? She's quite possessive. I wouldn't be surprised."

"You *know* his lover?" Tyler exclaimed. "Who was this woman?"

David blushed at the question, immediately sorry for the disclosure. He avoided eye contact. Rosaline instinctively knew he was about to lie.

"No clue," David alleged. "Professor Johnstone was cheating—not a well-kept secret. Most people suspected it was a student. Rumors were flying that this student had a dark side. I'm a law student, not an investigator or a judge, but if I were investigating this case, I would identify the scorned lover, whoever she is."

"Makes sense, David," Rosaline conceded. "We'll reach out if we have more questions, will that be okay?"

"Sure. I feel better for having talked with you guys. Here's my number. Can you text me, please? There is a criminal, a possible serial killer lurking about on campus. I don't want this person to see or hear me talking to you."

David left his number and exited the office. Rosaline glanced at the note. The handwriting seemed familiar.

Before she had the chance to determine where she had seen it before, Tyler's words interrupted her thoughts. "I will admit that his behavior creates suspicion; he lies at times. His relationship with the widow gives him a motive. But he's a law student with his whole life ahead of him. Never been in trouble. I can't believe he's capable of this."

"You know him better than I do. I can see you're fond of him. But don't let feelings cloud your judgment. He is still a primary suspect. He thinks he's in love with the victim's widow. Love triangles have been the center of murder plots for centuries, Tyler. I wouldn't be shocked to find out he's the killer."

"I understand, Roz. Perhaps I'm blinded by my feelings for the boy, but my gut tells me he's not our guy. Having said that, we must find out about this reconciliation thing. Were Kevin and Catherine going to try to make a go of it or had they decided to divorce? The answer to that question changes the suspect pool."

"Unless the actual perp had no clue and answered the question as he or she saw fit. In any event, we need to establish a connection between David and Lindsey. How does he know she's the lover? Or, is Lindsey not the only one Kevin was sleeping with?" Rosaline theorized.

"Huh?" Tyler was confused.

"Who's to say that Lindsey was the only woman Kevin was cheating with? Was he cheating on Lindsey with someone else? Or, did someone else come first? Jealous of Catherine *and* Lindsey?"

Tyler cradled his forehead in his hands. "My head is spinning. How do investigators do this? Every time I think we have things figured, someone else pops up. Makes me nauseous. Besides, David can't identify the so-called other woman."

"But he lied to us, Tyler. The lie was too obvious to ignore. Why would David unload the truth the way he did, unburden himself, and then lie about that? I think this is important. There has to be a reason. He's obviously covering for her, but why? They must have some sort of connection. I suggest we talk to Lindsey again, face to face.”

“Think she’ll be more forthcoming this time?”

“Let’s hope so. I’m going to contact Charlie at this point. He’s a former cop and a great private investigator. Hopefully, he’ll be willing to help. And, by the way, I’d like to question Lindsey solo; she respects me. First, though, I want Charlie to evaluate the case and help me formulate questions for the interrogation.”

“Okay by me, Roz. Whatever gets the job done. I defer to your expertise and good judgment.”

“Charlie? It’s Rosaline Maxwell. How are you?”

“Rosaline! Wonderful to hear your voice. Doing well?”

“Absolutely. How about you?”

“Great! I have a lot of time on my hands. Used to being busy. Now, I’m just bored, with one exception.”

“Oh? What’s that?”

“I bought your book and had time to read it. It’s a fascinating study, one that cops should be quite embarrassed about.”

“So, *you’re* the one who bought it. I’ve been wondering who it was. You’ve solved one mystery today.”

“Ha! You’re still a funny lady. Seriously, though, I’ll bet sales are brisk.”

"I wouldn't say 'brisk,' but I'm holding my own. As to the cops, I want you to know that I didn't write the book to embarrass cops. I wrote it to inform people that 'conviction of crime' doesn't automatically translate into 'guilty of crime.' No system is perfect—we are human— humans make mistakes from time to time. But we *can* try to learn from our mistakes. The book teaches techniques to prevent or reduce wrongful convictions and incarcerations."

"And prevention is vital. No one should serve time for something he or she didn't do. I learned a lot. How's the book tour going?"

"It's not. I got sidetracked. That's why I'm calling. How bored are you?"

"That's a loaded question. What do you have in mind?"

"Do you remember Tyler Guthrie?"

"Sure do. The school president, right? He was in the news recently, right? They say he killed someone."

"Fully exonerated. I took the bull by the horns, defied local law enforcement, and *proved* his innocence. I should add his story to my book. Tyler is why I suspended the tour."

"Didn't realize you became a private eye. How about that?"

"I didn't become a private eye. As a matter of fact, I'm probably way out of my realm. I worked hard, stuck with it, and proved Tyler's innocence. But I haven't solved the case."

"Proving someone innocent is no small feat, Rosaline. Pat yourself on the back. Glad it worked out for Tyler. Now, what's this got to do with me?"

"As you noted, Tyler is the college president. The victim was *his* employee and his death happened on *Tyler's* watch. Tyler, for obvious reasons, doesn't believe in the local cops. He wants me to continue to investigate. I got lucky, but things are heating up, out of my league. I sense a possibility of danger. I'm told you recently retired, but . . ."

"You need some professional help."

"Exactly."

"You're in luck. I finished your book. I'm bored again and looking for something to do. This sounds like the ticket."

"Are you sure? I don't want to interfere with your new-found boredom."

"Interfere away! Tell me all about the case."

Rosaline spent the next forty-five minutes providing Charlie with every minute detail, including the two anonymous notes and the recent conversation with David. She also broached the strategy of Charlie being the front man of a three-person truth squad. He was eager to do it.

"It might be dangerous, Charlie," Rosaline warned. "I don't know if the threat was real, a prank, or someone trying to stop us from investigating. The idea is to keep your involvement on the down low. We will plan—you will implement. The killer continues to watch us but won't have a clue about you."

"I've chased killers in plain sight and lived to tell about it."

"That's terrific, Mr. Macho, but never on my watch. If something happened to you, I would not be able to live with myself."

"I can handle myself, Roz. Skills don't erode in six agonizing months."

"Can we please try this my way for a while?"

"Yes, but I'm a big boy, Rosaline, and I don't like anyone threatening my friends. It's your case and your decision, though. I'm willing to try it your way, at least, in the early stages. When and where do we start?"

"We insist on paying you, Charlie."

"I insist on being paid. I usually charge four hundred a day, plus expenses. For you, and because you are alleviating my boredom, I'll do it for two hundred a day."

"Tyler and I appreciate it, Charlie. I suggest we have an introductory meeting. You and Tyler can get acquainted, and I'll bring my files."

"Okay by me. When do you want to do it?"

"Tyler just got released from prison. He's still on leave. The sooner the better."

"Tomorrow? Breakfast or lunch?"

"How about brunch? Eleven-ish? That little diner in Harbor Springs?"

"Works for me."

"I'll check with Tyler. Assume we're on unless I tell you otherwise. Thanks for doing this!"

"What are friends for? Sounds like you've done solid work on the case, but a new pair of eyes never hurts, even if they just provide a new perspective."

"True. See you tomorrow. Bye."

"Bye, Roz."

That evening, Rosaline called Tyler and filled him in on her telephone call with Charlie. Tyler sounded relieved when he found out a pro would soon be doing the heavy lifting. Rosaline was concerned about the perpetrator following one of them or the other.

They decided to take separate routes to neighboring cities, park their cars, and ferry across to Harbor Springs. Tyler would drive to Petoskey and take a Little Traverse Bay Ferry to Harbor Springs. Rosaline would drive to Bay Harbor and take a Little Traverse Bay Ferry across to Harbor Springs. They would meet up at the diner at eleven.

The following morning, Rosaline was up early. Her route would horseshoe around the lake for about fifteen miles to Bay Harbor. The ferry would then return her where she came from. *Who'd be dumb enough to do this?* She reasoned no one would follow after she boarded the ferry. She would remain vigilant and terminate the meeting if she sensed a tail. Tyler promised to do the same for his shorter trip to Petoskey.

The subterfuge was exhilarating. Rosaline saw no familiar faces, no vehicles for any extended time in her rearview mirror, and was reasonably certain that no one tailed her. She walked into the diner early at 10:30 in the morning. She was the first to arrive.

About fifteen minutes later, Tyler walked in, wearing a Detroit Tigers baseball cap, low on his forehead. Dark sunglasses completed his 'disguise.' He scanned his surroundings, acting like the guy in a television show being chased by the cops or the crook who believes someone is following him. After satisfying himself that no restaurant patrons were about to sneak up on or attack him or Rosaline, Tyler walked over to the booth where Rosaline awaited, and sat down.

"Good morning, Roz." Tyler smiled, distracted, continuing to scan the room.

Rosaline laughed. "Love the disguise! Did you behave like this all the way to the diner?"

"Laugh if you wish, but this is a weighty situation. Did you take the ferry like you said you would? How are you any better than me?" He challenged.

"You're absolutely correct. What time is it?"

"About 10:55."

"He should be here any minute."

"Tell me about this guy."

"His name is Charlie Granger. He's an ex-cop, first in Detroit, then Lansing, and, finally, in Charlevoix. If you ever pictured the quintessential cop, Charlie would fit that picture. Big guy, about 6' 1", 6' 2" or so, late 60's, early 70's. Was once well-built but probably had too many donuts. He's got a full head of beautiful white hair that would make younger man jealous and a pair of the most beautiful blue eyes you've ever seen."

"Like that?" Tyler pointed to a man walking in the front door. The man waved to the table, smiled broadly, and walked toward them. Rosaline waved back, gushed with delight, stood, and awaited the man's arrival.

"Charlie! You look terrific! Haven't aged a bit. Did you lose weight?" The pot belly was gone.

"I did. Can't dine with one of my favorite people without being in the best of shape. Come here, darlin'. Give this ole' boy a hug."

Charlie and Rosaline embraced as friends who haven't seen each other for a few years are prone to do. Rosaline broke away and turned to Tyler.

"Charlie Granger. Tyler Guthrie. Tyler, Charlie," she made the introductions.

"Pleased to meet you, Tyler. I understand you've been through the ringer lately."

"Pleased to meet you, too. 'Through the ringer' is putting it mildly. However, because of the hard work and dedication of one of your 'favorite people,' here, I've been fully exonerated."

"Congrats, Tyler. Rosaline is the best."

"Indeed." Tyler studied Charlie for a moment, fascinated by how accurate Rosaline's description compared to the actual

Charlie Granger, a cross between Sam Elliot and Dennis Farina. "Please Charlie, have a seat," Tyler pointed to the empty booth. Charlie sat down. "I took extreme precautions. No tails. How about you, Rosaline?" Tyler continued.

"Likewise. I'm no expert, but no one tailed me."

"No one knew to follow me," Charlie indicated.

"I understand Rosaline filled you in over the phone?" Tyler prompted Charlie.

"She did. As I understand it, you guys aren't satisfied with proving Tyler innocent; you want to identify the actual killer. Correct? But you're afraid that once you do that, and he finds out you're on to him, he'll try to silence *you*," Charlie summarized.

"Correct. So, the idea . . ."

"The idea is to continue your sleuthing, under the radar, run everything you find and you're about to do through me," Charlie interrupted. "You'll create the roadmap and I'll implement it. Because the killer may be following you, you want me to do the leg work while you do the brain work. Does that about cover it?"

"That about covers it in a nutshell. Tyler?" Rosaline nodded to Tyler.

"Nothing to add."

"It's a non-starter for me," Charlie burst their balloon. Rosaline was stunned. They discussed this last night and Charlie was on board.

"I don't understand, Charlie. You were fine, last night. What's changed?" A bewildered Rosaline demanded.

Tyler's mouth dropped open, subconsciously, listening to the banter between the two. He'd let Rosaline handle Charlie.

"Nothing's changed, Roz. But I'm not going to sit back and let you two amateurs determine protocol. I'll implement, just as we discussed, but I will also be involved in every other aspect of this thing, cool?"

"Absolutely! More than fine by me, Charlie!" Rosaline was relieved. "I didn't want to overstep or take advantage, with you being retired and all. You can do as much or as little as you would like. Tyler feels the same way. Don't you, Tyler?"

"Sure do. You can't beat experience and Rosaline and I have none."

"And I'm not about to permit two amateurs to chase a murderer with no experience and without my help, especially when one of them is an old friend. Like I said, that's a non-starter. Are we clear?"

"Crystal, Charlie, aye-aye, sir." Rosaline saluted. They all laughed.

"Okay, with that little nuance out of the way, let's discuss logistics and work assignments." Charlie got down to business.

"Sir, yes sir!" Rosaline saluted again, stifling her laughter.

"Cut that shit or I'll walk right out of here," Charlie snorted. "Who wants to bring me up to snuff?"

"I covered everything last night, but we can go over it again. I'll bring you 'up to snuff,' as you call it." Rosaline stifled a final guffaw, then regained her composure.

"Fine, but who do you have to bribe for service around here. Miss!" He signaled to a server. She approached the booth. "Round of coffees for me and my friends, here? And some menus, please?"

Two hours later, Charlie Granger was fully briefed, everyone's appetite was satisfied, and all were ready to take on a murderer.

Chapter Sixteen

The days were growing colder, and Rosaline snuggled into a warm, button-down coat as she prepared for her discussion with Lindsey Parker. Lindsey's schedule delayed the meeting, so Rosaline had plenty of time to discuss and outline the pending interrogation. She had a plan for approaching Lindsey and was glad Charlie was on board. While everyone agreed that Charlie would take over the active investigation, Rosaline suggested, and Tyler and Charlie concurred, that her previous connection to Lindsey made Roz the logical choice to meet with the young co-ed.

When she spotted Lindsey approaching her in the park, a slight sense of panic arose in her. She wondered what it would be like to have one of those earbuds that the agents wore on the FBI shows. Charlie would be in her ear, directing the conversation. Unfortunately, however, not today.

As Lindsey drew near, Rosaline was taken aback by her her appearance, dark shadows under her eyes and significant weight loss, coupled with a lackluster demeanor, devoid of her former enthusiasm, light, and energy. Kevin's death hit her hard, motivating Rosaline to work even harder for justice, hoping it might ease the young girl's suffering. Lindsey approached Rosaline, and the two friends greeted each other.

"How are you, Lindsey? Are you doing okay?"

"I look terrible, Judge Maxwell. You don't need to sugar coat things for me. I confess things haven't been going too well. I've been having these terrible nightmares, which make sleep difficult. I can't concentrate on my studies and my grades are tanking. I keep thinking of Kevin, lying there in that stairwell. I miss him so much."

Rosaline immediately thought of David and his suspicions about Kevin's unknown lover. Was Lindsey racked with guilt or remorse for having killed the man she loved? Rosaline studied the young co-ed. *She's too demure, too in love with Kevin, too vulnerable to commit such a heinous crime.* Rosaline decided Lindsey was the victim of a broken heart.

"I'm sorry for your loss, Lindsey. And, please, call me 'Rosaline.' Losing someone you love is difficult enough, but when that person is a murder victim? Who can prepare for such a tragedy?" Rosaline empathized.

"It's the most difficult thing I've ever experienced. How will I carry on? Everyone sees me struggling. They try to understand, offer to help, but I can't tell anyone why I'm spiraling downward. They think I'm clinically depressed or something. I can't tell anyone about the affair. They'd all hate me for it. You're the only one I can talk to, Judge . . . er . . . Rosaline.

"Everyone thinks Catherine is broken-hearted, and if they find out about the affair, they will blame me. Their relationship was a farce—she was cruel, cold, and heartless, a horrible wife to Kevin. Yet, she's the one who everyone supports and pities, while I suffer in solitude. It's just not right!" She burst into tears, then wiped them on the lapel of her lilac coat, pulling it tighter around her, like a soothing blanket.

Brightly colored autumn leaves fell around them; ducks swam in the lake. The grass was slowly browning, but the park was cheery, providing a pleasant distraction from Lindsey's circumstances, as the two women wandered farther down the dirt path, into the woods. The bright, crisp day clashed against the darker conversation they were beginning to engage in. Rosaline stuck to Charlie's script.

"I'm right there with you, kid," Rosaline began. "It seems incredibly unfair that you were devoted to him, made him happy, yet she receives everyone's comfort and consideration. I can see you are in immense pain. I wish I had a magic wand. I'd wave it all away."

"You *do* help me through, Rosaline," Lindsey advised. "Talking with you makes me feel better. At least someone is listening, compassionate about what I'm going through, and sees my struggle.

"You make me feel like I'm not crazy for feeling this way or overreacting for missing him so much. And I do miss him! I'd do anything to see his face, feel his touch, hold him in my arms, just one more time. I'd love to be able to fix things, save him from the monster in the staircase." Tears welled up in Lindsey's eyes—

she seemed on the verge of a breakdown, as Rosaline gave her a moment to collect herself.

"I understand what terrible regret feels like," Rosaline consoled, harking back to a few ghosts in her own past. There were things she would take back. She spent many long hours learning how to forgive herself and trying to move forward. "Beating yourself up helps nothing and takes you nowhere. It just contributes to an endless cycle of grief. You don't deserve that, Lindsey.

"My advice? The best thing you can do is move forward. What would Kevin want for you at this point? You're a young woman. He'd want you to be happy, live your life. Wouldn't he?"

"Yes, he would. But it's difficult without him. How can I live when the man I love is dead? This is so terribly unfair."

"It certainly is, Lindsey. But you are strong. I can tell. You're more capable than you think you are. Are you willing to do something to find closure?"

"Do something?"

"Yes. Help me and Tyler. We're doing everything we can to identify the responsible person. You were closer to Kevin and more involved in his life than either of us. Are you willing to answer my questions completely, openly, and honestly so I can track Kevin's movements in his last days? If we understand what was happening in his life at the time of his death, we can catch the person behind his murder. Kevin deserves justice."

"But I *have* helped you, Rosaline," she pointed out. "I've answered every question you and Mr. Guthrie have asked me. I've even acknowledged that we had an affair. I've helped in every possible way. What more do you need?"

"I need complete candor, Lindsey, and an answer to one more question. Can you do that for me?"

"If it will help find Kevin's killer? Anything! What's the question?"

"What is your relationship with David Barkley?" Rosaline floated.

Lindsey blushed, looked away, uncomfortable with the direction of the conversation. She paused. Rosaline awaited additional lies, preparing herself to prod the truth out of her young friend.

"Our relationship is rocky. We're on the outs, right now. We don't talk much these days—we've gone our separate ways. You see, David was my boyfriend before Kevin. We were together, once upon a time."

That David was Lindsey's ex made too much sense. Did Lindsey end things with David to take up with Kevin? And did David know Kevin was the reason? Clearly, David was not completely truthful about the relationship. Was everything a lie?

"When was this, Lindsey?" Rosaline queried. "And what caused the relationship to end?"

Lindsey contemplated the question as they continued to walk through the park. Rosaline noted falling leaves, dead grass, and flowers, and thought about spring. Dead grass and flowers regrow and bloom in glorious splendor in the spring, the circle of life. Not so for human beings.

"I'm going to sound awful, here, Rosaline. I'm not usually like this, but before Kevin, I was always respectful of relationships. I would never be disloyal to any partner, and would never carry on with this one, while dating that one. But it was different with Kevin. What we shared was exceptional, intoxicating, the connection of all connections. When I met him, I *had* to pursue the relationship. I was not about to let the perfect relationship pass me by."

"I understand how it is when you find the love of your life. This is still a no-judgment zone, Lindsey. I just want the truth."

Rosaline wasn't just blowing smoke Lindsey's way. She truly didn't blame the young college student. She blamed Kevin Johnstone for abusing his status, encouraging the child, occupying space in her head, and making her think he had true feelings for her, instead of honestly admitting he was using her.

She also blamed Catherine for similar conduct, taking advantage of a young student, and manipulating him as a pawn to be used to distract her attention from her asshole of a husband. She discounted the possibility that either Kevin or Catherine truly loved their young partners but decided that challenging Lindsey about this was pointless and would cause her to clam up.

"I was with David when Kevin and I met," Lindsey admitted. "We were together for over a year. I never intended to be disloyal to him. I thought I loved him. In fact, at the time, I thought he was the man I would marry.

"Kevin was my teacher. I never expected any type of relationship to develop, unless you call teacher-student a relationship. But after I started his class, we kind of connected. I can't explain it, but there was a chemistry there, an immediate spark. I did not expect it to blossom as it did, but about a quarter of the way through the semester, Kevin and I began to see each other outside the classroom. Innocent touch became illicit touch. Before I realized what was happening, I was cheating on David."

The revelation was stunning. If David knew that Lindsey was cheating with Kevin, that was a solid motive. First Kevin stole the woman David loved, then he hurt her, then he repeated the behavior with Catherine. How much could one young man take?

Rosaline played the scenario out in her mind. David kills Kevin, reasoning that he deserved punishment for Lindsey's betrayal and Kevin's deceptive behavior toward Catherine. With Kevin out of the way, David could choose between Lindsey and Catherine. Or, perhaps he might comfort and carry on with both.

"Did David know about your affair with Kevin?"

Lindsey blushed with shame. She nodded.

"First, he was just suspicious. Apparently, I gave off vibes—it's hard to hide true feelings. One day, I stayed after class to see Kevin and we had a rather prurient conversation. David was eavesdropping outside the door. He barged into the office and confronted us. It was awful! He was angry and hurt. It broke my heart to see him like that. It was one of the worst days of my life.

"I should have been honest with David, broken up with him when I started seeing Kevin. Instead, I cheated on him. It was shameful. I rationalized my behavior at the time by telling myself that Kevin was married. If he decided to patch things up with his wife, I'd still have David. Part of me treasured that relationship, too. After all, we were once very much in love. We might have rekindled the flame at some point. I was stupid and selfish. David paid dearly for both."

Lindsey stopped, turned to Rosaline, burst into tears, and fell into Rosaline's arms. The younger girl's body sank into the older woman's embrace. Lindsey squeezed Rosaline tight, as she convulsed in tears.

"You have to forgive yourself, Lindsey," Rosaline counseled. "Yes, you made bad choices. You were selfish, to be sure. But everyone makes bad decisions at some point in their lives. We hurt the people we love; the people we love hurt us. We're human—we make mistakes—sometimes those mistakes cause pain to others. All we can do is try to learn from them and do better in the future, apologize, offer to make amends, and move forward. But we must also forgive ourselves. It is useless to constantly beat ourselves over our heads with our mistakes. Let this go, Lindsey, or it will tear you apart. Move on."

Lindsey pulled away from Rosaline and pulled out a tissue. She dabbed her eyes and took a breath.

"I appreciate the kind words," she sniffed. "I have definitely learned my lesson. I would never do anything like that again. I will never have an affair with a married man, never cheat on anyone. I have apologized to David and tried to make amends. Whether he can ever forgive me is up to him, although I can understand why he wouldn't.

"I've made a mess of things and I hate myself for it. But I am trying to be a better person. Forgiving myself is part of that process, but it is the hardest part."

"You bet it is, Lindsey. And I'm here if you need someone to talk to. I mean it. Okay?"

"More than okay, Rosaline. I will definitely take you up on that one of these days."

"May I ask a couple more questions?"

"Fire away," she attempted to smile.

"What was David's reaction to the revelation?"

"Terrible," Lindsey conceded. "He broke up with me, of course, on the spot. He also threatened to expose Kevin, persuade the board to fire him, and otherwise ruin his life."

"But he didn't, did he?"

"No, he didn't," Lindsey scrunched her face, confused. "Strange, isn't it? I was terribly concerned about it. I thought Kevin would be fired and it would be my fault. I panicked, but Kevin was surprisingly calm. He promised to have a conversation with David. Then, he came to me, told me he had talked to David, and said we did not need to worry about him any longer."

Rosaline recalled witness accounts of Kevin's penchant for blackmail. *Did he have something on David?* That would make sense. Perhaps blackmail was just one more reason why David wanted Kevin dead.

"It's interesting, now that I think about it," Lindsey admitted. "I didn't consider it at the time. I relied on Kevin. He excelled at managing crisis situations. He was a talented mediator, after all, and I thought that's what he was doing. He had a way with words."

"I'm sure you can see why it now seems suspicious." Rosaline paused, allowing her comment to sink in. "Lindsey, this is a difficult question, but it has to be asked. Do you think David is capable of harming Kevin?"

"Perhaps," she conceded, her voice almost a whisper. "David? A murderer? As impossible as it sounds, I can't deny that the circumstances suggest it is possible. He does look guilty, doesn't he?"

"Let's investigate further, include him or rule him out. If David is the perp, we must make sure he's punished and do what we can to keep you safe."

"I appreciate that, Rosaline," Lindsey agreed. "Everyone needs closure. We also want to be sure that the right person is punished."

"Amen to that," Rosaline agreed. The two women sat down on a park bench, enjoying nature and the sudden calm of silence. Rosaline happened to glance down at Lindsey's freshly manicured nails.

"What a beautiful shade of polish. What's it called?"

"It's my go-to color, passion pink. First time I've had them done since Kevin died. I broke one earlier, so I repaired it evened the rest out. That's why they're shorter than usual."

"Beautiful," Rosaline gushed, trying to take Lindsey's thoughts to more pleasant things. "The coat is a perfect pairing."

Their conversation morphed into a discussion of fashion and other mundane 'female' things. Rosaline was pleased to see Lindsey recovering a bit of her buoyant personality as they walked back to their cars. This bit of 'girl talk' was a pleasant diversion from the case.

They parted and Rosaline got into the RV and drove away. When she stopped at a traffic light, she pulled out the number David had given her. Once again, she considered the handwriting and suddenly realized why she recognized it. She was now hesitant to call him.

Chapter Seventeen

Rosaline returned home to compare the writing on David's name and number to that on the various notes she received. She was correct. David's handwriting was a match to the first letter, pointing the finger at Lindsey for an alleged affair. But it was not a match to the letter threatening her. The handwriting was not the same.

Rosaline, back in her lakefront home, reclined in her favorite chair, contemplating her next move. Clearly, David was aware that Kevin and Lindsey were having an affair. He was attempting to direct the authorities toward Lindsey. Revenge? Take out Kevin and make Lindsey the fall girl? Two birds with one stone. He once loved her. Was he angry enough to set her up for a life sentence in prison?

The handwriting on the second letter was not a match, though. Perhaps David was working with someone else. Perhaps the partner was Catherine. Were they in this together? He wrote the first letter. Did she write the second to confuse anyone paying attention? Rosaline needed to obtain a sample of Catherine's handwriting. She couldn't just ask Catherine for a sample. She needed to be discreet about it. If she and David were willing to kill Kevin, they would not hesitate to do the same to her if they determined her a threat to their freedom.

The danger was obvious. She was gambling with her own life, for the purpose of exposing the slayers without alerting them she was on to them. Tricky situation, she needed to include Charlie. She decided to take a drive to clear her head, then pay a visit to Charlie.

While Tyler was her number one point of contact, she was more comfortable with Charlie's objectivity and experience. She felt lost, perhaps Charlie could help put her back on the right path and provide insight into her next steps. She backed out of the driveway and onto the road. She stepped on the brake, but the RV continued to roll back into the road. She panicked for a brief moment but realized that her speed was insufficient to cause injury if the RV collided with something. Suddenly, a car came barreling down the road, blasting music, the driver paying no attention to the road in front of him. He headed straight for the RV, oblivious of the danger.

Rosaline shoved the transmission into drive. It jerked, reversed course, and started back toward her driveway. She tried the brake again, no luck. She shifted the RV into neutral, grabbed the emergency brake lever, and pulled up with all her strength. The huge vehicle came to a sudden stop. Her belongings flew out of storage places, broke or clattered on the floor. The car zoomed by, music blaring, the driver oblivious to the danger he narrowly avoided.

Rosaline sat still in the driver's seat, breathing hard, willing herself to calm. As she began to relax, she turned off the RV and hopped out of the captain's chair. Outside the vehicle, she kneeled and peeked underneath. A dark puddle was forming. Rosaline was no vehicle repair expert, but she was certain that someone had cut her brake line. She walked into the house and called Charlie.

"Hello?"

"Charlie? Rosaline. Are you busy?"

"No. What's up?"

"My brakes stopped working. I believe the line's been cut. I might be paranoid, but can you come over and check them out?"

"Stay right there, Roz," Charlie urged. "I'm on my way. Call 9-1-1, now!"

"Are you sure? Maybe I hit something."

"Too much of a coincidence. Do as I say. I'll phone a friend, a mechanic, and meet you and the locals in a few minutes. And watch for anyone or anything suspicious. Understood?"

"Sir, yes sir," Rosaline saluted.

"Not funny, Roz. Might be an attempt on your life."

"Sorry. Humor is my number one coping mechanism. I'll behave. See you soon?"

"I'm already in the car and on my way."

"You're a treasure, Charlie Granger."

"So are you. Want me to stay on the line until I arrive?"

He was scaring her now. "That's not necessary, Charlie. Hang up and I'll call 9-1-1."

She made the call, told the dispatch operator what happened, and a squad car soon arrived at her home. Charlie and his mechanic friend pulled up at the same time. She thought about those Hollywood movies where the hero is driving along and realizes his brakes don't work. Someone is trying to kill him. Just before the car falls off the cliff, the hero jumps out of the vehicle, rolls around at the edge of the cliff, and narrowly escapes death.

If this was deliberate, was the person trying to scare her or kill her? Perhaps it was a threat to back off. Perhaps it was just a mechanical defect. She would find out soon enough.

She was now officially terrified. Was someone trying to kill her? Was her private probe worth risking her life? Tyler was exonerated. Would this person stop threatening her if she stopped investigating?

Rosaline was foolish to think she could investigate the incident without risk. Her safety mattered too, didn't it? Why should she concern herself with who killed Kevin Johnstone? Simple and complicated at the same time. She made promises to people, promises of justice. She would be breaching them if she backed out now. Besides, the killer might pursue her whether she stopped her search or not. She'd discuss things with Charlie. He would be her calm in the storm. She was quite pleased she decided to call him.

Charlie walked in the door with the mechanic and a Harbor Springs cop.

"We checked the brakes, Rosaline. The line was deliberately cut. I believe the intent was to scare you, not kill you. The perp figured you'd hit the brake while backing out of your driveway. Still, this was a message of some sort."

The mechanic completed a report for the officer who, in turn, interrogated Rosaline for an hour or more. Rosaline disclosed her recent activities, delving into Kevin's death, and her criticisms of Remer and his team. She had to exonerate Tyler. Remer was certain he was guilty. And when she proved her friend's innocence, there was a heartfelt apology, but no significant progress in identifying the actual killer. The cops were going nowhere fast. She bragged that she had more information than they did.

The reluctant officer took it all down. Rosaline was now worried that she made a new enemy: Detective Remer. The officer promised to keep tabs on her home, send a car around from time to time. Then, he and the mechanic left, and Rosaline made a pot of coffee for her and Charlie. As they sipped the warm liquid, Rosaline told Charlie what she was thinking. She had written everything down. She had a suspect in mind but needed to confirm the person. However, she had reservations or doubts. None of this was worth risking her life or Charlie's.

"Is it legal?" Charlie asked.

"Questionable," Rosaline opined. "Depends on the judge. Some judges would rule for us, some against. I'm not at all sure what the Michigan Court of Appeals or Supreme Court would do.

"It's a drastic step, but I don't see another option. Unless we expose this dude, something horrible might happen. The killer might strike again."

"I like the idea. And I'll handle the implementation, just like we talked about. The killer will never see it coming from me. All I worry about right now is your safety, Roz. Understood? I say the risk is worth the potential reward, but not at risk to your safety. I'll handle this."

"I'm so glad I reached out to you, Charlie. I feel better already. I've got to update Tyler."

"I'll handle that, too, Roz. Tyler might be in danger, as well. We must assume you're being watched, just as you thought when you arranged the meeting at the diner," Charlie warned. "You've done a fantastic job, better than anything the local cops have done on this case. But it is time to turn things over to a pro."

"You?"

"Me."

"My knight in shining armor. Okay, Charlie. I'll do what you say."

"Wonderful! Tell me everything you're thinking, and let's get this show on the road. Your safety is my number one priority. While solving this mystery is a distant second, I see no point in waiting any longer. I suggest we implement things as early as tomorrow evening. Is that okay with you?"

"Sir, yes sir!" Rosaline saluted.

"I told you, soldier. Cut that shit out!"

Chapter Eighteen

T he following evening, Charlie drove to Catherine's house. Rosaline and Tyler drove what Charlie called the 'follow vehicle.' Both were excited to wear an earbud, listening to Charlie bark out safety instructions to his small surveillance team (just like those FBI shows on television). The follow vehicle was a precaution. If all hell broke loose and Charlie shouted 'mayday' into their earbuds, Rosaline or Tyler was to call 9-1-1 and summon the cops to the scene.

Rosaline wore dark clothing. It was dark outside, and she was nowhere near the house. No one could spot her or Tyler, yet she felt vulnerable like she might be spotted at any moment and there was no true way to avoid danger.

She began to second guess herself. What they were about to do was clearly illegal. If she was the presiding judge, she'd throw the evidence out as the fruit of the poisonous tree. On the positive side, this wasn't an official, government sponsored operation. Would private citizens be held to the same standards as public officials? If caught, what type of punishment would they face? She and her two friends might have wiggle room, depending on the judge assigned to the case. *How many private citizens plan operations like this one?* After several agonizing minutes, she decided to give her nervous system a rest and leave things to Charlie.

Charlie approached the house, also wearing dark clothing. He extracted the threatening note from his glove compartment. He'd soon have a comparison sample of Catherine's writing, obtained through an illegal break-in of her premises. If Catherine was home and had a gun, she was entitled to protect her home. Charlie wondered if he should involve Remer and his team. A voice sounded in his ear.

"Are you there, Charlie?" Rosaline buzzed.

"Yes, Roz. I told you. Stay off the coms unless there's an emergency."

"But I wanted to try these babies out and, at the same time, give you a pep talk of sorts. I don't want to cause you trouble. You just retired. Perhaps I should do this, not you."

"Nonsense, Rosaline. I told you I would do it and I'm doing it. Besides, you're paying me, lady!"

"I'm writing the check, right now," she laughed. "Please be careful, Charlie. I'm having second thoughts. How do we gain entry into the house?"

"Here's a thought—I'll just knock on the door and ask her for a writing sample."

"Smartass. Please, tell me you're kidding. She doesn't know you. We should go together. How about that? I'll keep her busy while you make up an excuse to go to the bathroom or something. If she lets us in, it's not breaking and entering."

"That actually has merit, Roz. And a judge may view things through rose-colored glasses if we entered the place legally. Either way, I've got your back. What do you want to do?"

"I want the evidence to be admissible. I think we should do this my way."

"Okay, I'll alert team members who aren't on the com. Where are you? I'll pick you up. Tyler can monitor the whole thing instead of you. Are you game, Tyler?"

"Sir, yes sir," Tyler barked.

"Oh, brother!" Charlie moaned.

Ten minutes later, Charlie and Rosaline pulled up in front of Catherine's home. They walked up to the front door and knocked. No one answered. Charlie gripped the doorknob and turned it. Rosaline listened as her heart pounded in her chest. The knob turned. Unlocked! Charlie quietly pushed the door open.

"Anyone home?" He called. No answer. No one was home. Rosaline breathed a sigh of relief, then immediately felt panic again. *What if someone comes home while we're here?* Officers would be called to the scene of a B & E, she decided. They were taking a huge risk and she became profoundly sorry she involved Charlie. As they entered the house, a faint light came from somewhere inside the house. "Hello?" She called out. "Catherine? Anybody home?"

Charlie was satisfied that no one was home. He told Rosaline to stay put and greet anyone who walked into the foyer. Her story was to be that she came to talk to Catherine and found the door open. Suspicious of foul play, she entered the home, discovered no one was there, and decided to wait for Catherine to return home. Charlie would find another way out of the house.

As she stood in the foyer, she heard Charlie moving about the house, strange noises, steps up a staircase and on the upper floor, creaks, doors, and drawers opening and closing. Rosaline felt like they'd been there for hours.

She began to breathe heavily, panicked, sure that something would happen, an alarm would sound, and the place would be surrounded by cops. *We're going to jail!* If Catherine came home and saw her standing there, what would she do? Rosaline was completely exposed, completely at Catherine's mercy. *Stick to the plan,* she told herself.

She heard Charlie ascend a flight of stairs. Carpet absorbed most of the sound of footsteps. She again heard the sound of a search, door and drawers opening and closing, Charlie was moving quickly and quietly from room to room. She wondered whether he found anything. She wanted to get the hell out of there.

Charlie Granger crossed from the master bedroom into a small office. He stepped inside and shut the door behind him. It was pitch black. He illuminated the flashlight on his mobile phone, found a small lamp, and flicked on the light. His mission was to find a copy of Catherine's handwriting and compare it to the threatening letter that Rosaline had received. Roz was convinced they'd be a match and that Catherine would become a solid suspect. If they didn't match, no harm, no foul, they would go in another direction. No match would mean that David and Catherine were probably innocent.

A large, maple, roll-top desk stood in the middle of the room. It was immaculate, obviously not a working desk, or, possibly, the desk of a neatness freak. Everything was in place. Picture frames with smiling faces of children adorned the surface. Pens were placed in a cup designed for that purpose, and several documents were neatly stacked in the middle, as though someone was preparing to review them.

Charlie sat down in the swivel desk chair, picked up the papers, and began to leaf through them, wondering if they might provide insight into the woman that Rosaline had described. As he continued to review them, he realized how revealing these documents were.

The first set was bills and late notices. Johnstone was a ten percenter. Why would anything be late? Beautiful house, expensive cars, an extravagant lifestyle—people have been murdered for less. Living beyond a couple's means often strained the relationship. He'd seen this too many times in multiple scenarios. Late notice after late notice confirmed Charlie's suspicions. Creditor demands were piling up. Catherine was feeling the pinch.

He moved to the next stack of papers and discovered that Catherine had devised a solution, a way out of her late bills and crushing debt. These were applications for benefits due under a hefty life insurance policy, one whose beneficiary was Catherine Johnstone, with an obscene amount of money payable to the widow upon Kevin Johnstone's death. Catherine would never want for anything, ever again.

Charlie was anxious to show the forms to Rosaline and snapped photos of them with his cell phone. He had been led to believe an affair was the motive here, but here was a solid, alternative motive. *She killed him for the insurance money! How many times have I seen that one?* She was pissed at her husband for the affair, pissed that he neglected the bills or spent money on his cute little girlfriend. Kevin's death assured her custody of the kids and the resources to live happily ever after with her young law student. Was he a co-conspirator?

Still, he hadn't found what he came for, a sample of her handwriting. He continued to flip through the papers, trying to locate a handwriting sample or, at the very least, a copy of her signature on some important document. After what felt like a lengthy search, he found a document signed by both Kevin and Catherine. He pulled out Rosaline's note and compared the two. The handwriting was not a match.

Charlie wondered if Catherine altered her handwriting on one document or the other but was also aware how difficult it was to mask nuances. Catherine did not write the note. David didn't write the threatening note but did write the one that implicated

Lindsey. Thus, either he was also innocent, or he had a partner and the partner wrote the note.

Charlie secured photos of all relevant documents and bounded down the stairs to show Rosaline his treasure trove of evidence. Apparently, Catherine and David were innocent, and Rosaline was back to square one. As he reached Roz's side, they heard a noise at the front entrance. The doorknob began to turn.

Chapter Nineteen

Charlie put a hand over Rosaline's mouth, lifted her off the ground, and physically dragged her into the family room, behind the sofa. If Catherine found them, she'd likely press charges and they'd be arrested. Charlie could probably explain away his own behavior, but he couldn't risk Rosaline's reputation.

"Mom?" A young boy's voice called out. "Are you home?"

Charlie and Rosaline stayed still behind the couch, hoping against hope that the child would leave when he discovered no one was home. Rosaline felt like an idiot. She never considered the children when she concocted this ridiculous break-in. She betrayed Charlie, put both of them at risk for criminal charges, all to obtain evidence against a grieving widow who was likely an innocent victim of the crime, and not its perpetrator.

"Mom?" he called again. "I need to ask you a question. It's important."

Charlie and Rosaline remained hidden and quiet. Rosaline again felt her rapid heartbeat, silently wondering if it was loud enough for the child to hear. She tried to keep her breathing steady, but it was quick and unmanageable. If the child drew near, he'd likely sense their presence. Charlie was cool and calm—he acted like the experienced professional that he was.

Luckily, the boy gave up, leaving without much of a fuss. "Always nagging us to turn the lights off," he grumbled. "Can't even remember to do it herself."

He flicked off the light and the two home invaders heard his feet padding down the stairs. Rosaline's sudden nightmare continued. *Was Catherine somewhere in the house?* Rosaline was beside herself. If Catherine was home, sneaking out the front door was out of the question. The boy's call might have enticed her from wherever she was.

Charlie remained calm, searching his memory of the house for a quick and easy path to escape. He silently cursed himself for not turning off the light—if Catherine was somewhere in the house, she might come to investigate why the child found the light illuminated. *She can't be home! We called out when we came in.*

Charlie lifted his head over the back of the couch and scanned the family room. A large door wall led to a patio in the backyard. He ducked back down and faced Rosaline, silently pointing to the door wall and motioning for her to follow him. He willed her to maintain her wits and poise. If they were discovered in the house, they would have a lot of explaining to do, probably to the local authorities.

As they rose to start toward the door wall, the front door lock tumbled, and the door opened. They quickly ducked back behind the couch. A woman's voice, Catherine Johnstone, called out:

"Hello? Anyone home?"

"Down here," the boy shouted from the lower level. "I'll be right up."

Charlie and Rosaline heard his feet running up the staircase.

"You left the office light on," the boy informed his mother. "If I did that . . ."

"That's odd. I don't even remember going in there this evening. Are you sure?"

"Yes."

"Weird. Let's just be on guard tonight. Just in case . . ."

"Just in case, what?" the boy's voice responded, somewhere behind where Catherine was standing.

"Just in case," she repeated. "Time for bed. How was the game?"

"Awesome! We won in overtime."

"Must have been exciting."

"It was. Hey, where's Brooke?"

"Your sister stayed at Grandma and Papa's house."

"Good for her. You know, the game was not the same without Dad. He would have loved it."

"I'm so sorry about your dad, sweetheart. You're right, he would have enjoyed the game and some quality time with you."

"I miss him, Mom, so much!" The boy started to cry.

"I do too, my sweet boy. I do too," she sighed. "Let's go upstairs. You need to brush your teeth. I smell Coney dogs."

"They've got terrific hot dogs, Mom. And it's for school sports."

"Oh? *That's* why you eat those disgusting things?" She laughed. "Upstairs and brush those teeth, young man!"

Mother and son bounded up the stairs.

Charlie again lifted his head over the back of the couch and scanned the family room and hallway. He stood, walked over to the stairs, and listened. He heard a noise upstairs. A light went on and someone turned the water on. He returned to Rosaline's hiding place and motioned for her to follow. Together, they tiptoed to the patio door.

Charlie silently played with and disengaged the latch. He tugged on the door and it would not budge. He glanced down, toward the floor, and realized that the door had a floor peg lock, part of a home security set-up. To disengage, Charlie had to step on a button. When he did so, the latch made a loud popping sound. Charlie and Rosaline froze. *Did they hear that upstairs?*

Water continued to run in the bathroom. No steps were heard coming down the stairs. Charlie slipped open the door wall and discovered a locked screen. He sighed, rolled his eyes, and wondered whether this lock would also make a noise when disengaged. He flicked the lock, soundlessly, and started to slide the screen door open. It screeched as he did so and the two of them again, stopped in their tracks.

"Hello?" Catherine called from upstairs. "Is someone there?"

Charlie motioned for Rosaline to hurry out the door wall to the back patio. She did as she was told. Charlie trailed behind her, pulling the door wall and screen shut, just as the lights in the family room came on.

Charlie and Rosaline stood on the patio, in the darkness, watching, as Catherine entered the room. Obviously, Charlie was unable to lock the screen or the door wall from the outside. They watched Catherine walk toward them to the door wall. Rosaline froze in her tracks, terrified that Catherine would see them through the darkness. She gasped as Charlie picked her up and carried her further into the yard. They ducked behind a tree, just as Catherine pulled on the door wall and screen.

Her hand reached for a spot on the family room wall, and an outside light illuminated the patio. She surveyed the backyard and called out. "Anyone there?"

Why do people do that? Charlie asked himself. *What would they do if the intruder answered?*

The two trespassers remained crouched behind the large oak tree, waiting for Catherine's next move. Would she enter the backyard? If she caught them, what would they do? Admit they were snooping, searching for clues, and try to persuade Catherine not to call 9-1-1?

Charlie knew nothing about Catherine, but Rosaline had had a few encounters with Kevin's widow. She did not seem to be the most forgiving person or someone who would take kindly to a couple of idiots breaking and entering her home, perhaps endangering her children. Rosaline was an attorney and author, Charlie an ex-cop. How would a B & E look on their resumes?

"I know you're there," she called out. "If you come out now and identify yourself, I won't call the police."

Rosaline looked over to Charlie who motioned her to stay and be still. Catherine waited a few more seconds and closed and locked the screen and door wall, leaving the patio light illuminated. Luckily, the rather dim light did not reach their hiding place behind the huge oak. Charlie watched Catherine walk into the kitchen and pick up the phone. She continued to stare out at the backyard but did not dial the phone.

Charlie centered Rosaline in front of him and began to walk backward, continuing to use the tree to conceal their presence. This part of the yard was not fenced, and they soon backpedaled into a neighbor's backyard. As they continued to backpedal, the home security motion detector illuminated the yard with bright lights.

Catherine saw the neighbor's lights flick on and turned again to the yard. She thought she saw a figure or two in the yard, but whoever or whatever they were, they were quickly gone, probably scared by the lights. *Deer?* She put down the phone, turned off the family room lights, and walked back up the staircase.

Meanwhile, Charlie and Rosaline bolted between the two homes behind the Johnstone residence and raced toward the street. But they were not out of danger just yet. Charlie's car was parked in front of Catherine's home. "Take a breath," Charlie whispered, trying to calm Rosaline down. "Focus."

"Focusing," Rosaline willed herself to relax. "That scared the shit out of me! I'm so sorry, Charlie, I forgot about the kids. Dumb mistake. That's why I reached out to you in the first place. This breaking and entering stuff is way above my pay grade!"

"Nothing to be sorry about, Roz. You were almost a pro, but we are not in the clear yet."

"What do you mean? W-why not?" Rosaline stammered.

"My car is parked in front of the Johnstone home."

"Shit! I forgot about the car! What do we do?"

"Mrs. Johnstone and I have never met. And, besides, whatever she thinks she saw or heard, it was in the backyard, not the front. But she has met *you*. I want you to stay on this block and wait for me. I'll get the car, come back around, and pick you up."

Rosaline was panicked at the prospect of being left by herself, in the street, but she willed herself to keep her emotions in check. She did not want Charlie to sense her fear. She nodded, and Charlie took off jogging to the corner, turned, and disappeared from sight. Rosaline never felt more vulnerable in her life. She was certain that a patrol car would come speeding down the street, shining one of those spotlights in her criminal face. She'd be arrested, charged, and her writing career would be over before it started.

Instead of a squad car and a spotlight, Charlie Granger's car rounded the block and headed toward her. Charlie flicked his bright lights at her as he approached. He pulled the car to a stop alongside Rosaline, leaned over, and pushed open the passenger door, motioning for a frozen-in-place Rosaline to hop in. Rosaline jumped in the car and expelled a loud sigh. She felt like she'd been holding her breath for the entire evening.

"Are you okay?" Charlie queried. "Well, that was loads of fun. How do you like surveillance and B & E?" Charlie kibitzed.

"I've officially retired from my life of crime, effective immediately!" Rosaline exclaimed, wide-eyed.

"Oh, come on! Don't be so hard on yourself. You never panicked. I'm the one who screwed up. I made all the noise and I left the light on!"

"I forgot all about the kids. Stupid, stupid, stupid!"

"Listen to me. Give yourself a break. There are no perfect operations. Look on the bright side. We got what we came for and we didn't get caught."

"When the kid walked in, I just about peed my pants! Good thing you were there to pull me behind the couch."

"Hopefully you didn't leave DNA on the floor."

"Very funny, smartass! I was terrified. If I didn't soil my pants then, I must have when Catherine walked in."

"How about when the door wall lock clicked, and she came back down the stairs?"

Rosaline was into Charlie's game, now. "Or when she turned on the patio light and opened the door wall. I thought she was going to come into the yard and take a peek behind the tree."

"What about the neighbor's security lights? I think I peed my pants, too!" Charlie laughed.

Rosaline laughed, grateful to Charlie, not only for his funny and calming demeanor but for getting her out of the mess she created.

"Oh my *God*, Charlie. What would I have done if you weren't with me? I'd probably be explaining myself to the cops or sitting in a jail cell."

"Like I said, I'm the one who left the light on and made all the noise," Charlie reminded her. "Besides, the evening was not a waste of time. I've got interesting news for you."

"What's that?"

"The widow is not our killer. No handwriting match—she did not write that letter."

"Are you sure?"

"I'm sure. I not a handwriting expert, but I am as sure as I can be. No match here, the widow is innocent."

"Then who was it?"

"I'm don't know. David wrote the note about Lindsay. Perhaps he had another partner and that person wrote the threatening note. This has been a rough evening, why don't we call it a night and regroup in the morning?"

"Rough? It was terrifying! Nerve-wracking! How did you do this for a living?"

"Well . . . I didn't, actually. As a cop, I obtained search warrants and court orders and did things by the book. I didn't break into people's houses, but this was fun!" He chuckled.

"Yeah, loads of fun. Can we stop at the emergency room or a twenty-four hour clinic on the way home and check my blood pressure?"

"All kidding aside, Rosaline, you performed like a seasoned veteran tonight. I'm sure you were scared, but what concerns me is that we still don't know who's been threatening you. We're a *team*, do you understand me? We will identify the perp and obtain justice for this Johnstone fellow, your friend Tyler, the widow, and everyone else affected by Johnstone's death. He may have been a prick like you've told me, but no one deserves to die like that."

"I agree and that's why I am so pleased to have you on board. We *are* quite the team, don't you think? I can't wait to find the killer and be done with this case!"

"Amen, sister, amen!"

Chapter Twenty

Charlie dropped Rosaline off, watched her enter the home, turn on some lights, and disappear into the back rooms. He scanned the area around her house and saw nothing. Satisfied, he drove off into the night.

Kevin Johnstone's killer watched from a distance as Rosaline went into the house, wondering if Rosaline was focused on Catherine. Of *course*, Rosaline would pay Catherine a visit. Catherine was the widow—she could be guilty, just as the murderer intended. The couple was quarreling and there was that huge insurance policy, which would go to the kids if she got locked up for life. No one acquainted with this couple would lose a moment's sleep if Catherine was punished for Kevin's death.

Catherine's children needed someone to watch over them in their parents' absence. The grandparents were wonderful people. They checked all the boxes. If Catherine went away for life, the children would be in good hands.

But, would Catherine go down for the crime? Was there enough evidence against her? The investigating officers didn't seem to think so. They were reluctant to even consider her a suspect. If things continued on the present course, was anyone a more likely suspect than anyone else? Was there enough evidence to arrest anyone?

I'm dubious. It's annoying, but I suspected the cops would be clueless, their probe fruitless, a never-ending search leading nowhere, wasting everyone's time, focusing on all the wrong suspects.

Even if they didn't charge Catherine, eventually, these lazy officers would give up, consider the murder a cold case, with no apparent resolution. Everyone, including the local fuzz, would return to their lives and businesses. Kevin Johnstone would become a footnote in local history, forgotten by everyone, except, perhaps, his children. The cops were pathetically inept. The killer was sure their insistence on targeting Tyler as the murderer would make this the perfect crime.

And Tyler would have gone down if Rosaline Maxwell hadn't shown up. Now I must contend with this new guy, Charlie what's-his-name. Together, he and Rosaline were cause for concern, far more intelligent, vigilant, and determined than the investigating cops. In fact, Rosaline exonerated Tyler when the cops were too lazy to properly investigate the case.

Rosaline will never give up. She's a problem. I don't want to kill again. Shit, I didn't want to kill at all. I didn't intend to kill Kevin and I don't want to live in fear of Rosaline for the rest of my

*life. Or Tyler Guthrie, or this Charlie guy—that's no way to live. I
need peace of mind.*

The murderer watched Rosaline and Charlie boldly walk
up to Catherine's front door earlier that evening, impressed at their
tenacity, their willingness to sneak into the house, and boldly
search for evidence linking Catherine to the crime.

*I had the whole thing worked out, be rid of Rosaline
Maxwell, once and for all.* If Rosaline was caught in the house,
she'd have her own problems with the law. She'd be watched by
the cops, perhaps even charged, and would be unable to continue
with her little private inquisition.

But three unfortunate events screwed things up. First, the
kid came home while Charlie and Rosaline were in the house. The
killer did not want to involve the kid and couldn't call the cops, as
intended. Second, Rosaline stopped reviewing things on her own
or with that amateur, Tyler Guthrie. Charlie was smart,
professional, and too dangerous to screw around with. Third,
Catherine also came home. There were just too many unknown
factors inside that house.

*I watched the house, hoping that the kid or his mother
would discover Rosaline and Charlie and call the cops. Instead, I
waited, for hours it seemed, only to have this Charlie dude come
around the corner, hop into his car, and drive away. Where did he
come from? Where was Rosaline?*

Charlie started his car and drove around the corner. The
killer drove the other way, lights off. Rosaline Maxwell stood in
the street, illuminated by the bright lights of Charlie's car coming
toward her the other way. And Charlie's lights lit up the car's

interior. *Can he see me? Shit!* The killer ducked under the dashboard as Charlie whizzed by. Apparently, he did not spot the running car, lights off, parked at the opposite corner.

Rosaline and Charlie escaped into the night and Catherine had no idea that someone broke into her home. Or, if she did, she had no idea who it was. The murderer watched the whole thing unfold, feeling hopeless and helpless from preventing the escape. If Rosaline had been caught, her relentless inquiry would have ended. *No such luck.*

Staying at a comfortable distance, the murderer drove behind Charlie up to Rosaline's house, watched as he dropped her off, waited for her to enter, and sped off into the night. *Something must be done about this woman. She must be stopped. I can't be locked up—I'll go crazy. I have to end this, as soon as possible!* The killer drove home in silent contemplation, trying to figure out what the next move should be.

Chapter Twenty-One

S leepless nights only made things worse. The murderer paced relentlessly, took sleeping pills, long walks in the woods, and tried anything to relieve the constant stress. *I'm not cut out to be a killer. Don't have the stomach for it. Not in my nature. Truly, this was more an accident than a crime.*

In the middle of another sleepless night, staring at the ceiling, the killer's mind replayed the stairway incident—angrily approaching Kevin, demanding the truth, demanding he come clean. At long last, Kevin told the truth—he deserved credit for that, but the truth was so abhorrent it was unbearable, too difficult to stomach.

What turns an ordinary, law-abiding human being into a killer? Being pushed to the brink, not being able to stand another person any longer, a desire to have the person shut his mouth, stop with the filthy lies, a slight push backward . . .

I thought he'd brace himself. Did I push him that hard? I just wanted the bastard to stop talking. This was a tragic, heat of the moment, decision. I didn't intend for him to . . . die!

But, die Kevin Johnstone did. The killer remembered, heart pounding, in total disbelief, glaring at Kevin sprawled on that stairway, life slowly oozing out of him, a confused expression of betrayal on his face, blood pooling around his head.

The killer checked Kevin's pulse, thought about calling the authorities, but, instead, left the area, ending up in a local coffee shop, plotting a cover story. *I can't have my life ruined over Kevin Johnstone. The others were right about him. He was an asshole, a terrible human being!*

The killer calmly left the coffee shop, walked slowly, didn't run, didn't wish to draw attention, stepping away from life's most terrible moment. The killer's eyes opened. *I never wanted to be a killer.* This was a never-ending nightmare, haunting every waking moment, slowly destroying heart and soul. And now, a new debate, what to do about Rosaline, Tyler, and Charlie. *How close were these three to finding the truth?*

There was still a possibility that they wouldn't uncover the truth, that there was no need to kill anyone else. What were the chances that this would turn out to be the perfect crime?

Good? Slim? None? Not none—the crime was anything but perfect. There was still a solid chance that the three of them could solve the case and identify the murderer. *They've probably determined that Catherine Johnstone is innocent.* That made the situation far more dangerous. Who would be their new focus?

Their new patsy? *Will they turn their attention to me? I can't let that happen.*

This was one of those reality television shows, *Survivor? Survival? What's the name of that damned show?* Like *Survivor*, this was a story focused on the survival of the fittest. If killing Rosaline, Charlie, or even Tyler Guthrie, procured security from prosecution, it would be worth the price. But was it worth the risk? Perhaps it would be better to leave well enough alone. Of course, investigators could have prevented all of this by ruling Kevin's death an accident. But even those idiots saw through that. Kevin's 'accident' was an abject failure. This time, nothing could be left to chance.

It is not difficult to purchase a date rape drug on the street. GHB, Ketamine, or Rohypnol, for example, are available, as long as you contact the right dealer and have the cash to make the purchase. While this particular dealer was suspicious of the pill quantity the customer sought to buy, he decided that a sale was a sale—he jumped on the opportunity for a shitload of cold, hard cash.

The pills were secured on a promise that they would not all be used on the same person. The murderer hated the idea of drug-related overdoses or similar incidents, but they had to be done. It was difficult to concentrate after the death of Kevin Johnstone— the murderer tried to accomplish simple errands throughout the day, in a vain attempt to stop thinking about the task ahead. It was nearly impossible to focus when all conscious thought defaulted to attempted murder.

Kevin was an accident. Can I carry out the murders of three people? I don't know this Charlie person, but Tyler Guthrie and Rosaline Maxwell are good people. What would they do if they needed to kill me to remain safe? When will this nightmare end?

A couple days later, shrouded in the darkness, a familiar car sat outside Rosaline Maxwell's home in Harbor Springs. Inside, the merchant of death sat ruminating about the status of things. Were the private sleuths so close to solving the crime that ending their lives was the only viable solution? *Am I capable of cold blooded murder? Is human life so easily discarded?*

Rosaline was not at home. The killer had been following the former judge for a while and was now quite familiar with her quirks and habits. A spare key was kept under a flowerpot near the front entrance. *In and out, quickly. She might be home any minute.* The killer walked up to the house, retrieved the spare key, used it to unlock the front door, and walked into the cozy, lakefront home. Rosaline had a nose for details. Everything had to be returned to its proper place.

Casually strolling into the kitchen, the intruder checked the cupboards and fridge, wondering what Rosaline typically consumed before bedtime. It had to be something that would dissolve the pill. While rummaging through the fridge, the killer spotted an opened bottle of wine. Would Rosaline drink wine that evening? *It's possible.* This operation needed to end, sooner rather than later, but it required patience. The killer took a calming breath, opened the bottle of wine, and dropped several pills into the bottle.

The killer had done no research, knew nothing about the drug, how long it would take to kill someone, how much was needed to accomplish the task. It was a calculated gamble, one that the killer hoped would pay off. *At least I don't have to watch her die, like Kevin.*

As the refrigerator door swung closed, a key entered the lock at the front door. At first, the killer froze, then bolted toward the back of the house, hoping to find an immediate hiding place. *What is she doing here so soon?*

The intruder entered what appeared to be a guest room. The little used room was not a bad hiding place. The killer got down on all fours, laid down behind a double bed, waited, and listened.

Rosaline rummaged through the fridge, muttering something to herself. The fridge closed, footsteps were heard, going up a short flight of stairs. The killer seized the opportunity, quickly rose and unlocked the bedroom window, pleased that it lifted without difficulty or sound. However, a fixed screen blocked the escape. The intruder pulled out a knife and silently carved up the screen, creating a large enough passageway to enable a smallish human form to climb out. The operation seemed endless, and beads of sweat dribbled from the killer's forehead and temples. Shaken and trembling, the killer ran off into the night, praying that Rosaline Maxwell would soon decide to drink a glass of wine, and gently fall asleep . . . forever.

Chapter Twenty-Two

Rosaline came down the stairs, certain she saw something move outside. Before becoming involved in the inquiry into Kevin's death, she would have chalked it up to a squirrel, rabbit, or raccoon. With a predator on the loose, safety was paramount, and very little escaped her attention.

She raced down the stairs, glanced out a back window, and caught a blur of lilac moving away from the house. In an instant, it was gone. She tried to focus. Something seemed familiar. *The color!* But where had she seen it before? She could not place the object or event, but it stood out in the cascade of greens and blues that surrounded the lake. Someone was out there, watching her. *But, who?*

Rosaline was overcome with panic. She felt dizzy and a bit nauseous, unsure what to do. She sat down on the couch, took a breath, and contemplated her next move. Willing herself to calm, Rosaline rose, grabbed her handgun and coat, and ran out of the house. As she exited the front door, she noticed that the spare key was partially exposed under the flowerpot. *Was someone in my house?*

She grabbed the key and used it to re-enter the home. She turned on several lights and roamed through the house, searching for signs of an intruder. She entered the guest room and saw that the window had not been shut all the way and the screen was damaged. *Someone was here!* She immediately conference dialed Charlie and Tyler.

"Miss me already?" Tyler answered, having just spent an evening with Rosaline. "What's up?"

A line began to ring in the background of their call.

"Are you conferencing someone?" Tyler asked.

"Charlie," Rosaline declared. "I think someone broke into my home."

Before Tyler responded to this terrifying news, Charlie answered. "Roz? Is everything okay?"

"No, Charlie, it isn't. I've got Tyler on the line on a three-way. Someone broke into my house. Can you guys come over here? I am in a panic. What do I do?" The normally brave, courageous Rosaline Maxwell burst into tears.

"Where are you now?" Charlie huffed.

"In my RV. In front of my house."

"Stay there. I'll be there in ten." Charlie assured.

"Me too," Tyler promised.

"Let's all stay on the line until Tyler and I arrive. Start the RV and lock the doors. If you see anyone or anything suspicious, put the RV in drive and hightail it out of there," Charlie cautioned. "The cavalry is coming. Do you want me to alert the locals?"

"Whatever you think best, Charlie," a shaken Rosaline gasped.

"Stay put and remain vigilant. Here we come."

A half-hour later, Charlie, Tyler, Rosaline, and two patrol officers stood in front of Rosaline's home. Blue and red lights lit up the area, flashing on neighboring homes, boats, and the vast lake on the dark horizon.

The house was lit up like a Christmas tree. Every light in the house was illuminated, and a forensic team was combing for evidence, prints, or DNA. They homed in on the flowerpot, front door, guest bedroom, and kitchen.

"What exactly did you see, Ms. Maxwell?" An officer queried.

"I saw a flash of color, moving fast or running, first toward the lake and then east, along the shore. I'm not sure what it was, but it was a shade of lilac I've seen somewhere before. I can't place it, though. I thought it was nothing until I saw the window and the screen. Someone was in my house," she shuddered.

She quietly scanned the area, sensing danger. Someone was out there. She searched the shadows, seeking that familiar flash of lilac, sick to her stomach. This had to end. A monster lurked somewhere in the shadows. She was certain of it. The murderer was watching her, awaiting another opportunity. She sensed she would be his next target.

She saw nothing, heard nothing, felt an eerie sense of dread. Whoever it was, the person had vanished into the night. Was this the killer or a simple burglar? Was her imagination getting the best of her? She was beginning to question herself. *Did I really see a flash of lilac? Where have I seen that color before?*

The forensics team completed their work. Nothing was missing. Perhaps Rosaline's sudden return home frightened the intruder out of ransacking the home. He apparently wore gloves because there were no prints on the front door handle, flowerpot, window, or damaged screen. They did collect a few droplets of liquid at the window, from which they might obtain a DNA sample. After the house was cleared, the crime scene specialists advised Rosaline she was cleared to re-enter.

Charlie continued to talk with the officers while Tyler tried to comfort Rosaline.

"I was so worried about you," he effused, as they walked inside together. "I can't believe this happened. What if this crook had come at you? Why would you chase after him? Something terrible could've happened. You must be more vigilant!"

Tyler seemed strangely pleased to soothe and lecture Rosaline for a change, rather than the other way around.

"You don't have to worry, Tyler," Rosaline promised. "Nothing happened and I'm perfectly fine. The cops think it was probably an intruder."

Charlie walked into the foyer at that point. "Yes, they do, but I've got to be honest, Rosaline. I'm not convinced. This is too coincidental, and I don't believe in coincidences."

"Coincidental how?" Tyler was confused.

"Someone killed Professor Johnstone and threatened Rosaline's life. Same person? Two different people? Someone she's met? A stranger? It's all a mystery. But this break-in is related to this case. I'm certain of it."

"He's right, Roz. And this guy didn't just threaten your life, he tampered with your RV. I think she needs protection, Charlie," Tyler opined.

"I'll arrange it, if it's okay with you, Rosaline." He turned to his friend and partner.

"Absolutely. This night has shaken me to my core. I'll be on my best behavior, do whatever you brave, strong men recommend," she murmured.

"Real funny, Roz. Will you take this seriously, please?"

"I am, Tyler. As I told Charlie, humor is the way I cope. I mean it, Charlie. I will gladly accept your protection detail."

"Wonderful. I'll arrange the detail."

Charlie went back outside, his phone to his ear, calling in the protection detail. Tyler and Rosaline walked into the family room and sat down on the couch.

"I'm glad you're following Charlie's advice. Protection is like chicken soup—it can't hurt. Better to be safe than sorry.

Someone threatened your life and tampered with your car. Now this break-in or whatever it was. Someone may want you dead. Can't be too cautious."

"I understand and agree, Tyler," Rosaline sighed. "I guess chasing after this person was a bit reckless. I should have called the cops. I'm just desperate for all this to be over. I want this guy caught."

"I understand. This is all my fault. I should never have involved you in the case. Should have called a lawyer and let him hire someone like Charlie to investigate. Gotten to the bottom of this without putting you in danger," Tyler repented. "I put you in danger and I will never forgive myself if something happens to you. Please be vigilant, listen to Charlie, and do whatever he says. This person is waiting for us to lose interest, perhaps. We need to outsmart him, whoever he is."

"I chose to help, Tyler. That was *my* decision, not yours. I'm a big girl and I can make my own bad choices. Besides, you'd still be rotting in a prison cell if I hadn't gotten involved, so, it was all worth it. I'll defer to Charlie from now on," Rosaline assured him. "I won't rush into danger or do anything stupid. I promise."

"I'm going to hold you to that. Want me to stick around for a few? Spend the night in the guest room?"

"I'd welcome the company," she smiled. "Would you like something to eat or drink while you're here? I have a fantastic bottle of wine."

"I'd love some wine," Tyler sighed. "My nerves are shot from all this shit."

"Mine too. You've earned a glass." Rosaline opened the fridge and grabbed the wine off the shelf. "I don't think I'm going to indulge. I think I'll have a cup of tea, instead. My stomach's a bit upset from all this stress."

"Totally understandable. How about I make the tea while you pour the wine?"

The two prepared each other's drinks before sitting down on the couch together. Rosaline held her mug in both hands, wrapping her fingers around it for warmth. Tyler slowly sipped his wine, beginning to relax.

"Every time I think we're about to solve this thing, something unravels. I thought we had a solid lead on David's co-conspirator, but now I wonder whether he's involved at all," Rosaline bristled.

"David has great character. While love or lust can do strange things to people, I truly doubt he's a killer," Tyler offered. "He's never given off that kind of energy. I prefer to think the best of him, even if he is somehow wrapped up in any of this unpleasantness."

"I think you're probably right about David," Rosaline admitted. "So, who's left?"

"Not sure. What does Charlie think? Another student or professor? Someone who was carrying on with Kevin?" Tyler suggested.

"You were so right about Kevin, Tyler. Catherine, Lindsey, and another woman? What a stud! I thought he was charming—I had no idea he was a serial adulterer. Kevin's mistress is an ideal suspect. Some type of jealous rage? Lindsey and Catherine might still be in danger," Rosaline speculated.

"Hell hath no fury like a woman scorned. It would seem that my friend Kevin was quite easy to fall in love with. He manipulates a woman into an illicit relationship. Lures her into his bed, whispers sweet nothings in her ear, convinces her that she's the one, above all the others," Tyler surmised.

"Until she finds out she's not," Rosaline suggested. "Someone like Lindsey, but this one is capable of murder because she hasn't yet fallen madly in love with Kevin Johnstone. What if she found out that Lindsey and Kevin were an item?"

"Or that Kevin was going to reconcile with his wife?"

"Something to consider, although that one applies to Lindsey, as well. Kevin really manipulated her. She was in love with him. Still, like David, I can't imagine her killing him or anyone else," Rosaline opined. "I've seen lots of cases in my courtroom where love makes people do crazy things. It's an unfortunate fact of life and a compelling motive. We have to consider all suspects."

Rosaline glanced at Tyler. Something was wrong—his eyelids began to flutter. He set down the wine glass, rubbed his eyes, and began to falter, having difficulty breathing.

"Are you okay?" Rosaline asked.

"Just tired, I guess," Tyler speculated. "And a bit queasy. Might I take a little cat nap on the couch?"

"Sure. You look unwell, though. Are you sure you're okay?" She rose to fetch Tyler a blanket.

Tyler opened his eyes and glanced around the room. It was spinning. He tried to rise but fell back onto the couch. "I'm really dizzy, Roz. Maybe this wine hit me hard or something. The room is spinning, blurry . . . I'm sick . . . not sure . . ." Tyler slumped back onto the couch and began to convulse. His eyelids fluttered. Rosaline screamed for Charlie, who came running into the house at full speed.

"What's wrong?" he cried.

"It's Tyler. Something's wrong with Tyler. Call 9-1-1!" Rosaline ordered.

She went to his side, shaking him, willing him to wake up. "Tyler? What's going on? Wake up! Say something! You're okay. Stay awake. Don't fall asleep!"

Tyler was barely semi-conscious, his body shaking, slightly. He was still breathing. Rosaline's entire world was crashing down around her. She heard Charlie's voice, explaining the situation to a 9-1-1 operator, but could not make out the words. When he finished the call, he touched her arm. She jumped, then listened as Charlie assured her that help would arrive soon.

Tyler's breathing was becoming labored. His body continued to shake. Saliva dribbled out of the corner of his mouth. She had never witnessed anything like this before. *How do I help him? How do I save him?*

She glanced at the quarter-filled glass of wine, sitting on the side table. *The wine!*

"Charlie! It's the wine! Someone poisoned the wine! The intruder meant it for me! But *Tyler* drank it. Oh, Charlie, it's the *wine*! Tyler is suffering a fate meant for me!" She burst into tears and fell into Charlie's arms.

"I've got it, Roz. I've got it. For now, we send the glass to the forensics team. Figure things out. Right now, though, I need you to remain calm and talk to these EMS attendants."

Rosaline did not see them rush in, towing a gurney.

"What happened, ma'am?"

"It's the wine. He drank the wine," she shouted, half-delirious.

"What about the wine?"

"It's been poisoned! Someone poisoned the wine!" she ranted.

"What kind of poison? What was in the wine?"

"She has no clue," Charlie took over. "Someone broke into the house tonight. I suspect that this person poisoned the wine."

"Please be okay. Please, Tyler! You must survive this so we can finish our work. Get justice, Tyler! Live! Get through this, for me. I can't do this without you!" Rosaline carried on.

"The police are outside," Charlie lifted her chin. "Come outside with me, Roz, and let these talented emergency people work on Tyler."

Rosaline didn't want to leave Tyler's side. She wanted to stay with him, encourage him to wake up, snap out of it. But his best chance was to allow the professionals to do what was necessary to save his life. Charlie placed his arm around her and led her out the front door, shaking. This was too much, like a never-ending nightmare.

An officer approached the two as they emerged from the house. His badge read 'Henderson.'

"Will someone please tell me what happened here tonight?" Officer Henderson demanded. His intense brown eyes bore into Rosaline's. He was a cop's cop, in full uniform, with brown hair cut short, military style, his demeanor all business, with a trace of citizen-friendly kindness.

"We had a break-in earlier," Rosaline advised.

"I'm aware, I was on that call, too," Henderson responded. "Is this related to the break-in?"

"Yes!" Rosaline cried. "The intruder poisoned the wine!"

"What makes you think that?" The officer challenged.

"Because Tyler drank wine and I didn't. The poison was intended for me!"

"Why would anyone want to poison you?"

Rosaline was hesitant to repeat the story. Her entry into the case was not popular with Detective Remer and company. They resented her interference with Tyler, even though she proved his innocence. But Tyler was suffering. Perhaps he was dying. He deserved their absolute best. He deserved justice. Besides, this was her house. If she was unable to provide an alternate suspect, suspicion might fall on her.

She glanced at Charlie, who nodded her to proceed. She told Henderson everything, soup to nuts. As she spoke, Tyler remained in the house with the emergency medical workers. She began to panic, again. She glanced at the front door and nodded toward it.

"Is Tyler going to live?" she blurted. "Please, tell me."

"Hard to tell at this point, ma'am. A few more questions and I will go inside . . ." Henderson's words were interrupted by a stretcher being shoved through the door of the house.

Rosaline dissed the cop and ran to her friend, *He's alive!* That was the important thing. Tyler was alive and being transported to an ambulance that would take him to a local hospital.

"Can we finish this later, Officer Henderson? I've got to go to the hospital," she insisted. "Please?"

Henderson nodded his assent and put away his notebook. He and Charlie began to chat, perhaps filling in blanks, leftover from Rosaline's sudden departure. Rosaline ran to the ambulance, waiting for the attendants to properly situate Tyler, and climbed into the van, terrified that Tyler might die on route to the hospital.

Chapter Twenty-Three

Rosaline sat in the hospital waiting room for what seemed like a lifetime or two, waiting for an update on Tyler's condition. She paced the room, then the hall, watching the clock, listening to it *tick, tick, tick*. She would not be distracted, her mind was too focused on Tyler and what she still believed was a life-threatening condition.

As she sat, then paced, sat, paced, memories flashed of the incident. Why did she offer him the wine? Why didn't she drink it herself? *He's got to recover from this . . .*

A doctor entered the waiting room and called: "Is anyone here for Mr. Guthrie?"

Rosaline called out and waved her hand in the air. "Me! Here!"

"Are you family?" the doctor requested.

"We're not related, but I am the only 'family' he has around here." Rosaline hand-signed quotation marks. "Talk to me, please?" She was frantic. "How is he doing? He's my best friend."

"*HIPPA* requires that I only divulge medical information to family members," the doctor insisted.

"Doc, please, I'm not asking for the gory details of his medical records. I'm only asking if he is going to survive being poisoned." The doctor's reluctance to talk to her was scaring her even more.

"Are you Rosaline?" the doctor asked.

"Yes . . . I am . . . wait a minute . . . who told you to call for Rosaline? Do you have news of his condition? Please?"

"I'm Doctor Richardson. Tyler gave me permission to talk only to you. I'm pleased to tell you that he'll make a full recovery."

Rosaline's heart soared. She reached out and grabbed the doctor, aggressively hugging him. When he extricated himself from the awkward embrace, he told her more about Tyler's condition. Tyler was a fighter. He'd survive this. He overdosed on a version of the so-called 'date rape' drug.

She became more determined than ever to put Kevin's killer away for life. She'd obtain justice for Kevin, Catherine, Tyler, and herself. *Poor Tyler.* He'd been falsely accused of someone else's crime, put in jail for no reason, and accidentally poisoned by a drug meant for someone else. How can one person be so unjustly targeted? The killer must pay for all harm caused. Everyone needed closure.

The doctor advised Rosaline to go home and rest. Tyler was resting comfortably and was not permitted any visitors at the moment. Rosaline stayed, of course. She had to see him as soon as he was permitted visitors. She continued to wait, as patiently as possible.

With nothing but time on her hands, she began to consider the evidence compiled in the case. Perhaps they were looking at things from the wrong vantage point. Tyler was framed, then poisoned—they might be looking in the wrong direction. They were chasing people connected to Kevin Johnstone. But what if the perpetrator had no connection to Kevin? What if the principal connection was Tyler? An elaborate ruse or smokescreen to ruin his life? Besides Kevin Johnstone, who hated Tyler Guthrie that much?

Rosaline wanted to rush into Tyler's room and ask him about this possible connection. Instead, she took out her cell phone and called Charlie Granger.

"Hello? Roz? How's Tyler?"

"He's doing well, Charlie. The doctor says he will make a full recovery."

"That's wonderful! Where are you? Still at the hospital? Do you need a ride or something?"

"No, Charlie. I appreciate the offer, but I'm going to stay and wait until Tyler wakes up."

"Okay, Roz, keep me posted."

"Charlie? I want to run something by you. I need your opinion."

"About what?"

"Do you think it's possible that Tyler has been the connection, all along? We've been looking at people connected to Kevin but look at all the grief Tyler has experienced."

"Interesting theory, worth a look, perhaps, but I have an important question."

"What's that?"

"The poisoned wine was in *your* fridge. There's not a reason in hell why the killer would have expected that *Tyler* would drink it. Seems to this old cop's brain that the target was *you*, Roz, not Tyler."

"The killer now hates us both. First, he frames Tyler for the crime. I push back and he decides to kill me—Tyler also—to end our search for the truth. Are we now too close for our own safety? You're a possible target, too, Charlie."

"As I've told you many times, Roz, I'm a big boy. Stop fussing over me."

"I'll concede that you're more than capable, but the more I think about it, the more certain I am. This isn't about any particular person. This is about my work on the Harbor Springs mystery."

"So? What? You want to stop? Let the cops do their thing and stay far away and safe? Just say the word and I'll shut this damned thing down."

There were too many questions and no easy answers. Rosaline had hit a wall and felt exhausted. Should they widen their net? Narrow their focus? Increase or decrease the number of ways to be defeated by this monster? She was frustrated, learning fast that loose ends were terribly difficult to tie up.

She wanted to be safe, craved for this to end. But she also desperately wanted justice. She'd never despised anyone like she despised this merchant of death. She wanted the person to pay for all the mayhem. She wanted this person to spend a lifetime in prison. She refused to stop now, despite the risks.

"No, Charlie. I don't want to stop. I *can't* stop, not until justice is done."

Seated in a hospital waiting room, waiting for Tyler Guthrie to regain consciousness, Rosaline plotted strategy with Charlie. She pulled out a pen and note pad and listed anyone who might have an issue with her or Tyler. Considering her age and legal history, the list was quite long. Charlie joked that, with all these enemies, it was surprising she lasted as long as she did.

Try as she might, however, despite the long list of potential revenge seekers, she could not find any that overlapped with Tyler. Was he framed to punish her somehow? Too elaborate and farfetched, she decided. But she reminded herself not to underestimate a criminal's capacity for cruelty.

Terrible people do terrible things, sometimes picking their victims completely at random. Countless criminals came before her, with pages of criminal records, a clear and long history of law-breaking behavior. Hurting another person, even killing one, was easy for certain types of people.

However, some cases involved unique circumstances, victims and family members who never considered the perpetrator capable of such depravity. Families destroyed by dark secrets, upstanding members of the community brought down by their double lives. She'd seen the shock and horror of those who never believed that someone close to them was capable of violent crime.

In fact, that reality is what led her to consider the possibility that Tyler might actually be guilty. He had motive, means, and opportunity. She was well aware of the human capacity to be blinded by one's own positive experiences with someone who is secretly a predator.

So, with Charlie's help, she decided to ignore the blinders, consider *anyone* capable of murder, and follow the evidence, to whomever it led.

"Fine with me, Roz. Who have you been blind to in this matter?" Charlie challenged.

The answer descended upon her like a ray of sunlight glaring through the dark night. She remembered the flash of lilac she saw behind her house during the burglary. She *did* see lilac, but not a *thing*, rather, a person, more accurately, an article of clothing worn by a person, the intruder, the deliverer of death.

"Someone broke into my house and poisoned the wine," Rosaline postulated. "But I came home, unexpectedly and the intruder ran out the guest bedroom window. But this person didn't run fast enough. I saw that familiar looking flash of lilac."

"Lilac?" Charlie was confused.

"Lilac," Rosaline remembered, with renewed confidence.

It was all so clear now. Rosaline recalled the lilac coat she complimented. And as she remembered she recalled other things. Her mind flashed back to Kevin's body in the staircase, to random things scattered on the floor near the body, Tyler's pen, for example, caused Remer to consider him the prime suspect. But *everyone*, including her, ignored the broken, chipped, pink nail, the one that linked the actual perpetrator to the crime scene. *Stupid, stupid, stupid! How could I have missed such an important clue?*

Rosaline was an amateur—new to this sleuthing stuff. But the Harbor Springs Police Department and Detective Remer ignored the importance of that small but vital piece of evidence, too. In fact, they were so focused on the pen, so sure it meant Tyler was the murderer, they completely missed the chipped fingernail. *Shame on them!*

She recalled complimenting Lindsey Parker on the beautiful lilac coat she wore to the book signing event. Later, she commented on Lindsey's unusual manicure, and the pink nail polish she called her 'go-to' color. Lindsey attended the book signing. Kevin was there, too. Perhaps Lindsey tailed Kevin. She might have walked with him to the staircase.

And this was the final piece of the puzzle. Lindsey's kind nature and feelings for Kevin were two factors that prevented Rosaline from viewing her as a prime suspect. She was manipulated by him, but when she spoke of Kevin, she was heartbroken. She missed him and claimed to be in love with him. Her words were tender. The look on her face when she spoke of him was not the look of someone who hated him enough to kill him. But, kill him, she did. *Why?*

"Complex triangles are often compelling motives for murder, Roz. How many spouses kill their significant others?" Charlie suggested.

Another lightbulb flashed in Rosaline's head. Perhaps Lindsey's overpowering love for Kevin was what drove her to commit the ultimate crime. Kevin decides, for the sake of the children, to reunite with Catherine. Did he end the relationship, right there, on that staircase? In a rage, Lindsey pushes him, not intending to kill him, but watches in horror, as he falls awkwardly to his death.

How ironic it was that the life of Kevin Johnstone, doer of bad deeds, serial adulterer, was snuffed out as he attempted to do the right thing. He professed loyalty to his wife and children, renewed his sacred marital vows, and attempted to become a better husband, father, and man. Lindsey must have been furious, emotionally distraught enough to commit the evil deed.

"Can we prove it, Charlie?" she questioned. "It's nothing more than a former judge's intuition. What proof do we have?"

"Did the cops preserve the nail? As incompetent as they have been in this case, they must have bagged and tagged the broken fingernail. That's forensics 101. I'm willing to bet that DNA will demonstrate that the pink nail belongs to your biggest fan." Charlie joshed.

"We also have the lilac at the break-in, matching her coat, which I'm sure the men in blue will soon possess after they exercise their search warrant."

"And, we have those droplets by the windowsill in your house. What if those are small dribbles of sweat or saliva? If Lindsey is the intruder, those will match the DNA from the fingernail. Put it all together and you have ironclad cases of murder and attempted murder." Charlie summed up the evidence. "Want me to call Harbor Springs and fill them in?"

"Not yet, Charlie. Can we meet somewhere? I want to be sure before I contact them."

"I'm sure, Roz. As a former copper, I'm as sure as I can be."

"I know, but would you humor me for a few hours? She's not going anywhere, and she has no idea we're onto her."

"You're the boss. I hope you know what you're doing."

"Pick me up at the hospital?"

"Your Uber driver will arrive in less than ten minutes."

Rosaline laughed. "You're the best, Charlie. I'm so happy I brought you into this. I couldn't have solved it without you."

"All evidence to the contrary," he conceded. "You would make a terrific private investigator. Ever consider a new career?"

"All this case has done is cause me grief. Why would I want to do this for a living?"

"That's an easy one, my dear."

"Easy? Okay, hot shot, why easy?"

"Because it's who you are. What's your book about, lady? Protect the innocent. Make sure the guilty are punished. Bring sweet justice to the victims. Gee whiz, how is it that Rosaline Maxwell is interested in a career that helps accomplish all three of those goals? Look what you did in this case."

Rosaline was stunned. Charlie was absolutely right. However, she had no time to consider the future. She'd think about it later. Right now, her focus was on finding Lindsey Parker. She needed to confirm her inviolable suspicion that the young co-ed was a cold-blooded killer.

Chapter Twenty-Four

C harlie retrieved Rosaline at the entrance to the hospital.

"Where to, lady?" He greeted her.

"Funny. You are a load of laughs today."

"I'm a happy guy, Roz. Granger and Maxwell, Private Dicks, Inc., is about to solve its first case."

"*Dicks*? Seriously? And why not Maxwell and Granger?"

"It's my firm and I have more experience. You should be happy I put your name on the door."

"I thought you were retired. I should hang my own shingle. After all, you said I cracked the case without you."

"I told you. I'm bored. Besides, who will keep you safe, huh? I've got a gun and I'm an excellent shot."

"That's a huge plus. Okay, if we do this, you can have top billing."

"How magnanimous of you, allowing me to head my own firm."

"You're welcome. Can we talk about the case, now?"

"Talk away. You're on a roll."

"First, I suggest we contact Tyler's office and ask his administrative assistant to text us a copy of Lindsey's class schedule."

"Excellent idea."

Rosaline was determined to make this case so ironclad that investigating officers would have no choice but to arrest Lindsey Parker for murder. Otherwise, she and Tyler might be looking over their shoulders for the rest of their lives. If she turned Lindsey in prematurely, and an arrest was not made, Lindsey would seek revenge, somewhere, sometime. Rosaline and Tyler would be forced to live in fear for years.

As Charlie drove toward campus, Rosaline's phone pinged with copies of Lindsey's and Raven's class schedules. Apparently, Rosaline's relationship with Tyler carried weight with his administrative assistant. They arrived at the school and headed toward an expected destination.

While they waited, Rosaline received a call from the hospital. Hastily retrieving the phone, she feared tragic news. *Tyler's condition has worsened. He has only hours to live. I will never forgive myself.*

"Mr. Guthrie asked us to give you a call. He's awake," the caller informed. "Giving the nurses a hard time, I might add."

"That's my Tyler," Rosaline sighed, relieved at the news. "Please tell him I will be there as soon as I can. There is something important I must do first. And tell him he will be severely reprimanded if he doesn't behave."

"I will definitely pass that along. The nurses will appreciate it," the caller indicated, with gratitude.

"Good news?" Charlie asked after Rosaline hung up the phone.

"*Wonderful* news!" She exclaimed. "Tyler's awake, alert, and being a pain in the ass to the nurses."

Charlie laughed. "I don't know him that well, but that's his prerogative. The customer is always right."

"I'm a judge. In legal matters, the customer is almost *never* right. That's why I've put so many of them in prison or summarily dismissed their civil cases."

"Point taken. What do you have in mind for this evening?"

Rosaline fiddled with a can of pepper spray in her purse, grateful that Charlie and Charlie's gun were with her. They began to walk toward Lindsey's dormitory. As they arrived, Raven pushed open the entrance door to head to class. She was surprised to see Rosaline but gave her a genuine, kind smile and greeting. After greetings and introductions were exchanged, Rosaline got down to business.

"I need to talk with Lindsey again. Something important. Is she around?"

Raven looked conflicted. "Lindsey isn't here right now," she responded. "I'm sure she'd be delighted to see you. She can't stop talking about your lecture and book. You're welcome to wait in the vestibule or on that bench, over there." She pointed to a bench just outside the entranceway. No way for Lindsey to avoid them, but sufficient for Rosaline to do what needed to be done?

"Would you mind if we waited in your room?" She floated. "It's kind of cold out here and there's no seating in the vestibule. I've got a bad foot."

Raven paused, considering what she viewed as an odd request. "She should be here soon— her class lets out at three. I guess it will be okay. Follow me."

She led them into the dorm and over to their shared room. Rosaline feigned a limp to buttress the notion of a bad foot.

"Make yourself at home. Lindsey won't be long."

"Thanks, Raven. I appreciate it."

"No problem."

Raven left for class and shut the door. Rosaline implemented phase two. Charlie continued to be impressed with her spunk. She walked over to Lindsey's side of the room and began to search her desk. They weren't cops on official business. They needed no warrant. There were no 'fruit of the poisonous tree' considerations.

After filtering through books, pens, note cards, and printer paper, with no results, Rosaline was becoming desperate. Lindsey would be coming home soon. She tried another drawer and found what she was looking for. The drawer contained files of her class writings, notes, papers, and short stories.

Charlie handed her the threatening note for comparison. While not identical, it was rather obvious that Lindsey had thought about handwriting comparison and attempted to alter or obscure her handwriting. Despite the effort, the samples were too similar to ignore. Rosaline was convinced that they were written by the same person. Charlie agreed.

Lindsey Parker wrote the threatening note. When considered with the lilac coat, the pink fingernail, the love affair, and her proximity to the staircase at the time of the murder, Lindsey was Kevin Johnstone's murderer. She was hiding in plain sight the whole time and bamboozled local law enforcement and Judge Rosaline Maxwell. Rosaline had to give her credit. She was behind it all and covered her tracks well, except for the pink fingernail and her inability to leave things be. Had she not gone after Rosaline and Tyler, she might have gotten away with the initial crime.

"Hardly on my radar screen," Rosaline had noted.

She grabbed the note and one of Lindsey's papers and placed them in her purse. She'd show the two samples to the crime lab. Next, she strolled over to the bathroom and retrieved Lindsey's hairbrush. Charlie marveled at her as she pulled out a plastic baggy, pulled hair out of the brush, skillfully placed the hair inside the baggy, and sealed it.

"What makes you think it's Lindsey's hair and not Raven's?" Charlie questioned.

"If you look closely like a woman would, the two girls have distinctly different hair colors and textures. This is Lindsey's hair. I'm betting my life on it."

"Well, that settles it, then. I'm just here for bodyguard purposes, anyway. You are the master."

"Not quite sure about that, but I am starting to embrace this private eye gig. I will turn all this over, ask Remer to do DNA testing on the nail, the droplets in my home, and these hair samples. You will be my disinterested witness. DNA will prove, conclusively, that Lindsey Parker is a murderess."

"Well done, Roz. Well done. I'll go get the car. Wait for me out in front of the building."

Charlie left, and Rosaline gazed around the room for one last time. It was like any one of the many dorm rooms across the country, housing hundreds of thousands of young students whose typical concerns were grades, future careers, parties, the opposite sex, drinking, getting high, and partying. *How many of these kids were cold-blooded murderers?*

As Rosaline turned to leave the room, the door handle turned. Rosaline looked at her watch. *It's too early—can't be Lindsey.* Perhaps Raven forgot something.

To be safe, however, Rosaline texted Charlie with a pre-determined emergency code word and the name 'Lindsey.' She fingered her pepper spray and waited.

Lindsey Parker walked through the door.

"Hi Rosaline," Lindsey chirped, happily. "I ran into Raven. She said you came by to talk to me. I was so anxious to find out what it was all about, I left class early."

Not a care in the world, Rosaline huffed. She was so calm and nonchalant, in fact, that Rosaline slightly dropped her guard. Apparently, Lindsey was unaware that Rosaline was onto her. At least, that's how it appeared at the moment. Rosaline hoped they would have a short chat and Lindsey would allow her to leave in peace.

"Just checking in, making sure you're okay," Rosaline explained, struggling to remain calm. "I'm not sure this is common knowledge on campus yet, but something terrible happened to Mr. Guthrie last night. I'm concerned that whoever killed Kevin Johnstone is behind what happened to Mr. Guthrie. We haven't unraveled the details yet, but Mr. Guthrie and I have both received threats.

"Considering your relationship with Kevin, I was concerned that you might become a victim, too. Have you had the feeling you were being watched? Anything suspicious happening in your life?" Rosaline was delivering an academy award performance. Lindsey seemed to relax. She nodded and stepped forward, looking totally exhausted.

"Yes, actually, there has been some suspicious stuff," she admitted. "I haven't approached you because I didn't want to put you in danger. Apparently, you're already in danger, though. Perhaps it might be safer to open up and tell you the truth. By the way, where's your friend? Raven told me you came with a man."

"Yes, Charlie Granger. He's an ex-cop. He's helping me look into Kevin's murder."

"Ex-cop, huh? Glad you have someone. I'm sure Mr. Guthrie is no help."

"Charlie's just down the street, over by the administration building. Went to get the car." Rosaline wanted her thinking that protection and detection were just around the corner.

"You said something terrible happened to Mr. Guthrie?"

"He was poisoned last night."

"Oh shit!" She exclaimed. "Pardon my French. Who would do such a thing to Mr. Guthrie? Hasn't he been through enough? Geez!"

"The same person who killed Professor Johnstone, I'm afraid. Anyway, I just got a call from the hospital, and Tyler will be fine. So, it's all positive news."

"Well, anyway, back to your question. I think someone is stalking me, or whatever the cops call it. I keep seeing this dark figure, lurking behind me. There was a threatening note taped to my door the night before last. Whoever wrote it threatened to kill me if I continued to talk to you and Mr. Guthrie about the case."

"My word!" Rosaline exclaimed. "That's awful. That happened to me, as well. It's terrifying. Did you save the note? I can have Charlie turn it in to forensics. A crime lab might find a fingerprint or DNA sample from it. Did you notify the authorities?"

"I was afraid to call them," Lindsey shook her head. "Besides, I don't have it anymore. I tore it up into little pieces and threw it away. I was too scared to even keep it around. It was torturing me. In twenty-twenty hindsight, I should have kept it."

The cat and mouse performances continued.

"I completely understand your visceral reaction. My note scared the hell out of me—I can certainly empathize with your desire to dispose of it, get that negative energy out of your life.

"How about this? I'll go out front, wait for Charlie, and you can tell both of us all about this over lunch. What do you say? I think we need to catch this person, so we can all feel safe again," Rosaline suggested.

The last thing Rosaline wanted to do was have lunch with Lindsey Parker. If Charlie tagged along and they were dining in a public place, she'd be a lot safer than she was now, trapped in a private dorm room with Lindsey. *If I can make it out of this room alive . . .*

"That sounds lovely." Lindsey smiled for a moment, then became distracted by a piece of paper protruding from Rosaline's purse. "What's that paper sticking out of your purse?"

Rosaline brushed it off. She shoved the paper into the depths of the purse.

"It's just some old notes," she fabricated.

Lindsey seemed placated until her eyes wandered to the mess on her usually organized desk. Her eyes narrowed on and glared at Rosaline.

"You're a liar," Lindsey accused. Before Rosaline had a chance to react, Lindsey pulled out a gun.

Rosaline raised her hands in surrender, eyes fixated on the gun. Lindsey was no expert—her hand shook nervously as she pointed it at Rosaline's heart. Pointing a gun and shooting someone you admire are not the same as pushing someone and having that person accidentally fall to his death. Even attempted murder by poison didn't require her to act and observe the horrible consequences.

As for Rosaline, she chided herself for her stupidity. She failed to consider that Raven might run into Lindsey, sent Charlie for the car, and came armed only with pepper spray. She underestimated Lindsey's resolve, never expected her to produce and aim a gun at her chest. *Where was Charlie?*

Lindsey's voice shook in a combination of fear and anger. "You betrayed me, lied to me!"

"I was hoping to *clear* you, Lindsey," Rosaline concocted, thinking as she spoke. It was difficult with a gun pointed in her direction and an unstable person holding the weapon.

"I came to talk to you," Rosaline continued. "I was going to ask you for a handwriting sample to clear you of writing the threatening note. I didn't think you threatened me, poisoned Tyler, or killed Kevin.

"But while I was waiting, I found some samples at your desk. I admit that I compared them and took them, but they *exonerate* you. I compared the writing and they are clearly written by two different people. You aren't the person who threatened me.

That means you didn't poison Tyler or kill Kevin. But you must put down that gun and let me out of here. Charlie will be here any minute."

Lindsey scoffed. "More lies, Rosaline? They don't suit you. Besides, you're a *terrible* liar. I see right through you. I'm not stupid. You uncovered the truth, But not the *whole* truth. Kevin's death was an unfortunate accident. I pushed him, true, but I did not expect him to fall down the staircase. That was an accident. I didn't mean for him to die. Hell, I didn't even mean to hurt him. Just one of those things—a little push, not much of one."

Rosaline was now officially terrified. If Lindsey was willing to admit to killing Kevin, the young co-ed had no intention of letting Rosaline go.

"I know you loved him," Rosaline retorted. "And I believe it was an accident. You're no cold-blooded killer." Rosaline hoped to woo the young woman by appealing to her own twisted version of the truth.

"Kevin's death was a tragic accident," Lindsey insisted. "This isn't me. I hate doing this."

"Then don't, Lindsey, just don't!" Rosaline implored. "You didn't mean to kill Kevin. And you didn't kill Tyler. He survived the poison. He survived! You'll serve time, but not too long under these unique circumstances. Sentencing guidelines favor situations like yours. I can explain everything to the authorities when you turn yourself in. I'll contact a grief counselor, so you can begin to think rationally again. But you must stop this, now, and let me go. I *know* this isn't you."

A million emotions played out on Lindsey's face. She was terribly conflicted. Rosaline believed in Lindsey. In her heart, she sensed the kid was not a natural killer. But Lindsey was desperate, and desperate people make irrational decisions.

"If I don't kill you, I'll go to prison," Lindsey pointed out. "I'd rather die than spend my life rotting in some prison."

"But killing me will also send you to prison, Lindsey. And for a much longer stretch. Raven knows I came to see you. So does Charlie, and Raven also saw Charlie. Are you going to kill them too? Where does this stop, Lindsey? You have to stop. They're going to find me in your room. Who killed me? Raven? I don't know her. If Charlie finds me here, dead, he will go to the police and they will hunt you down. They'll string everything together and you'll go to prison for everything. A life sentence. Don't you see? Please, Lindsey, please let me help you."

The desperation on Lindsey's face grew darker as she realized the truth of Rosaline's words. Her hands shook even more violently as panic overtook her.

Rosaline continued. "I'll talk to Tyler. I can try to persuade him to drop any charges. And I won't mention the gun to anyone. You can just turn it in and say you don't need or want one. I'll represent you in court and persuade the judge to give you the lightest sentence possible for Kevin, a great plea deal . . ." Rosaline had to pause, as Lindsey gasped and put the gun to her own head. Tears streamed down her face.

"There's no use," Lindsey cried. "You're right. I'm going to prison. I can't let that happen. I'd rather die. I can't do it."

Despite the terrible things Lindsey had done, Rosaline could not let her die. She was no more than a confused child, betrayed by a villainous con artist. *A child cannot lose her life over a scumbag like Kevin Johnstone.* Perhaps she'd change, be redeemed, even in prison. Rosaline needed to persuade her to see that simple truth.

"Lindsey, please, honey. I'm a former judge. I know how things work. It's not all bad. I can help you. Let me help. I'll negotiate a sweetheart deal. This isn't the end for you," Rosaline promised.

"And many people have made wonderful changes while incarcerated. They emerge from prison better people than they were when they went in. They have families, careers, full lives. They work hard, change, and do things the right way. They receive counseling. You can be one of those people, Lindsey. You can change your life for the better. You can live."

At that moment, a loud knock on the door interrupted their conversation. Lindsey glared at Rosaline, with anger and terror in her eyes.

"What have you done?" Lindsey was horrified.

Whoever it was, Rosaline had to act. If she failed, either Lindsey, Rosaline or the person at the door might be injured or killed. She decided she was willing to give up her own life to make sure that this did not end in further tragedy. Lindsey was nothing more than a young, confused, child.

"It's either Charlie or Raven, or another friend of yours. Are you going to put them in danger, too?" Rosaline challenged.

"What did I do, you ask? Nothing! You've been with me the whole time. Cut it out, Lindsey, now! Do you really want to shoot whoever is knocking at the door? What if it's Raven? Do you want her to walk in and see you holding a gun on me or to your head? Please, Lindsey, stop!"

Lindsey hesitated. She cared for her roommate. She lowered the gun and turned to see who was at the door. Rosaline reached into her pocket and stepped forward. Lindsey turned back toward Rosaline, with gun lowered, and was greeted with a shot of pepper spray straight into her face. The gun clattered to the floor, she cried out in pain and covered her face with her hands. Rosaline picked up the gun, ran to the door, and opened it.

Charlie, Raven, and several officers stood on the other side. Lindsey fell to the floor, hard, against her bed, hands covering her very painful eyes. Rosaline dropped the gun and the canister, as officers entered the dorm room. She raised her hands in surrender as tears welled in her eyes. She was safe once again.

Epilogue

"You are truly a *mensch*, Tyler Guthrie. Lindsey owes you, big time. This doesn't happen without you. Are you okay with the sentence?" Rosaline asked as she and her best friend left the courtroom.

"I'm fine with it, Roz. Lindsey is nothing but a tormented child, tossed aside by the asshole known as Kevin Johnstone. If anyone got what he deserved in this whole affair, it was him."

"You don't mean that, Tyler. I know you're angry. Yes, he sexually harassed one or more students. He's responsible for a scandal that rocked the institution to its core. But that's over now, and Kevin didn't deserve the death penalty for his admittedly abhorrent behavior, Tyler. Surely you agree."

"Close question. I'll concede the point if it makes you happy and you treat to hot fudge sundaes."

"Deal."

"Have you heard from Catherine? What's her take on the sentence?"

"I think she's okay with it, too. Probably lukewarm? Lindsey must face consequences, but the principal perpetrator, the person who set all of this in motion is Kevin Johnstone, may he rest in peace."

"Rest in peace? May he rot in hell!"

"Tyler! What happened to conceding the point?"

"Yeah, yeah, yeah. Blah, blah, blah. Rest in peace . . . *asshole*. Ten years is a very generous sentence, all things considered. I'm no lawyer, but aren't there multiple crimes involved here? She might have done time for each of them, right? I think it's fair. She didn't mean to kill Kevin but she sure as hell meant to cover up the crime. She was not thinking rationally, with the poison and the gun she pulled on you, but she was hurt and manipulated by the master of hurt and manipulation. She let me rot in prison and then poisoned me. I should hate her, but I don't. I'm rather sorry for her. I hope they provide the help she needs while she's in prison.

"I'm just happy we can live our lives again, without threats, without looking over our shoulders. I've been restored to my position as school president, my true passion. I'm more motivated than ever to help the school through this crisis, help teachers, administrators, and students heal, and put everything back on track."

"I love that positive attitude. I'm happy to see you happy. It's a gratifying feeling, knowing we can breathe again, out of danger."

"It sure is. Does your return to normal life mean you're going to resume the book tour now?"

"Yes, it's an important topic, the work of my life, and a great distraction from the Johnstone case and all the trouble that happened after I became involved. The one positive thing from all of this is that my book sales are through the roof! I will probably be answering more questions about the murder mystery in Harbor

Springs than about my book. My heart is still in this, and I am committed to this topic and this tour. I'll be leaving next week.

"I'll miss you. I won't be gone too long. I'll see you soon. By the way, I haven't told you yet, but I'm going to be around."

"Around?"

"Yes. Charlie Granger is unretiring. I'm going to go into business with him—Granger & Maxwell, Private Investigations. We're going to solve complex cold cases and obtain releases for the wrongfully incarcerated."

"Wow! That's terrific. May I join you from time to time? I enjoyed being a snoop."

"I'll ask Charlie."

"How long will it take for Charlie to be answering to you? Maxwell & Granger?"

"I already broached the subject."

"And?"

"He shot it down. Remember, Tyler, he's the one with the gun."

"Work your magic. You'll wear him down. Besides, don't forget, *he* helped *you* solve the crime, not the other way around. Meanwhile, as to your return to the book tour, I'm happy for you. You deserve a break after everything you've been through. You, quite literally, saved my life."

"I'm pleased everything worked out and the truth prevailed. As my book and research indicate, it doesn't always turn out that way. I'm relieved you're safe."

"Amen, Roz. Now, about those hot fudge sundaes . . ."

About the Author

Mark M. Bello is an attorney, social justice advocate, and award-winning author of the Zachary Blake Legal Thriller series. Mark also writes for legal and political content sites and hosts the legal themed podcast, *Justice Counts,* on the *Spreaker* network. A Michigan native, Mark and his wife, Tobye, have four children and nine grandchildren. For more information, please visit *https://www.markmbello.com.*

Books
in the Zachary
Blake Legal Thriller Series

L'DOR V'DOR –From Generation to Generation
(A Prequel Novella)

Betrayal of Faith (1)
Betrayal of Justice (2)
Betrayal in Blue (3)
Betrayal in Black (4)
Betrayal High (5)
Supreme Betrayal (6)
Betrayal at the Border (7)

You Have the Right to Remain Silent (8)

The **Zachary Blake Legal Thriller Series**
is also available in audiobook format.

Books in Mark's Social Justice/Safety Series for Children

HAPPY JACK SAD JACK — A Bullying Story

ONE THING OR TWO — ASHER'S DISTRACTED LESSON

Other Books by Mark M. Bello

L'DOR V'DOR –From Generation to Generation II

The Blake-Lewin Family Cookbook of Traditional Jewish Recipes

Connect with Mark

Website: https://www.markmbello.com

Email: info@markmbello.com

Facebook: MarkMBelloBooks

Twitter: @MarkMBelloBooks

YouTube: Mark Bello

Goodreads: Mark M. Bello

LinkedIn:

https://www.linkedin.com/in/markmbello

Subscribe to our mailing list and receive your *free copy* of

L'DOR V'DOR -From Generation to Generation

and other giveaways and other surprises.

To request a speaking engagement, interview, or appearance, please email info@markmbello.com